I grabbed for reverse and floored it. The Mustang lurched back about six inches, then crunched into a big Ford station wagon planted rock-solid behind us.

"Ambush!" I yelled.

It was already too late. Another car was hard against my door now. A fat man with a biker's hairy face grinned at me over a double-barreled shotgun aimed at my throat. The back doors of the van ahead opened. Another man, crouched inside, covered us with an automatic weapon.

I felt sick to my stomach.

RAFFERTY: FATAL SISTERS

W. Glenn Duncan

FAWCETT GOLD MEDAL • NEW YORK

Library of Congress Catalog Card Number: 90-90299

ISBN 0-449-14552-2

Manufactured in the United States of America

First Edition: November 1990

"Three fatal Sisters wait upon each sin:
First Fear and Shame without, then Guilt within."
Robert Herrick, *Noble Numbers*

PROLOGUE

Nine-year-old Eric Calmet to his mother: "Lookit the neat papers I found in the alley, Mom. It must be spy stuff. Codes and things. I'm gonna decode it!"

$$
\begin{array}{ll}
& \text{DS} \\
5/12 & 3 \times 60 = 180 \\
& 4 \times 50 = 200 \\
& 1 \times 85 = \underline{85} \\
& 465
\end{array}
\qquad
\begin{array}{l}
\text{BC} \\
4 \times 60 = 240 \\
5 \times 50 = 250 \\
1 \times 85 = \underline{85} \\
575
\end{array}
$$

465 — ($\$110$) — 575

$$
\begin{array}{ll}
& \text{DS} \\
5/13 & 2 \times 60 = 120 \\
& 5 \times 50 = 250 \\
& 1 \times 80 = \underline{80} \\
& 450
\end{array}
\qquad
\begin{array}{l}
\text{BC} \\
2 \times 60 = 120 \\
5 \times 50 = 250 \\
1 \times 80 = 80 \\
1 \times 120 = \underline{120} \\
570
\end{array}
$$

450 — ($\$120$) — 570

$$
\begin{array}{ll}
& \text{DS} \\
5/14 & 1 \times 60 = 60
\end{array}
\qquad
\begin{array}{l}
\text{BC} \\
2 \times 60 = 120
\end{array}
$$

. . . . .

Mrs. Nita Calmet to her son Eric, four days later: "How many times did I tell you today to get these papers off the table? Too bad, bucko, out they go."

1

CHAPTER ONE

I knew it was going to be one of those days as soon as Patty Akister walked into my office. She fidgeted awhile, then she asked me to find her husband, Sherm.

Sherm, the secret agent.

Uh-huh.

Patty was thirty-five or so, with a fresh, well-scrubbed look about her. She was a couple of pounds past plump, nudging comfortably into chubby, and it looked right for her.

Her hair was brown and curly, cut just a little too short to suit her round face. Either she needed a new beauty parlor or she wore it that way to please someone. Secret agent Sherm, maybe.

Patty Akister also had apple cheeks and wide blue eyes and perfect skin and a pleasant face that, on a normal day, would have smiled often.

Norman Rockwell would have painted her in the kitchen, busy and happy, with smudges of flour on her calico apron.

Patty Akister wasn't happy today, though. She was worried sick about poor Sherm.

"I'm afraid he's been hurt, Mr. Rafferty," she said. "Or captured."

"Captured," I said.

Patty's face fell even farther, and she twisted her dainty handkerchief. She had large hands and she gave it a pretty good twist. A watching chicken would have broken into a cold sweat, seeing that twist.

"Yes," she said miserably, "captured. Look, I shouldn't even be here. I promised Sherm a dozen times I would never tell anyone about his work, but . . . but he's never been away on a mission this long. I'm scared."

"On a mission," I said.

"I went to the police first," Patty said. "I thought maybe Sherm had an accident. You know, with the car. I was afraid he was stuck in a hospital, unconscious or something. But the police checked and he isn't. They asked me questions and filled out forms and all that, but, you see, I told them Sherm's cover story. I didn't tell them he's really on a mission."

"Mission," I said again. And why not? Conversationally I was on a roll.

"Yes. Well, anyway, then I decided to hire a private detective, because talking to one—talking to you—would be secret, sort of. Like talking to a doctor or a priest."

"A privileged communication," I said.

"Yes, like that." Patty nodded and looked hopeful for the first time.

In my line of work the tired old secret agent line pops up once or twice a year. I have never decided which group is the saddest: the husbands who invent that drivel or the wives who believe it. It's probably a dead heat.

But there was obvious anguish in Patty Akister's eyes, and it wasn't her fault she loved this jerk Sherm, so all I said was: "Which intelligence agency employs your husband?"

"I don't know," Patty said. "Sherm isn't allowed to tell me."

"Did he say where he was going on his, ah, mission?"

Patty shook her head and twisted the hell out of her handkerchief again.

Some of the phoney secret agents use the routine that way. *Sorry, baby. Hush-hush, need to know, top secret. Of course, if it was up to me . . .* But then again, some of them come up with dandy details. Three years ago I tracked down a carpet salesman who had told his wife he'd be gone to Mars for a week on a spy flight for NASA. I found him in a Fort Worth motel bathtub with a lady cabdriver. Maybe his rockets had a dead battery that morning.

I said to Patty, "How long is Sherm usually gone?"

"When he's on a mission, only a day or two. Usually he's back by Saturday. Late Saturday, sometimes. But he's always back by Sunday evening. Always."

"Have all his missions been on weekends?"

Patty nodded. Her curls bounced. "Yes. Only about once a month, though. Not every weekend. Well, he did have two missions one month, but that was unusual."

I said, "When did he leave on this mission? Saturday morning?"

"Friday night, right after supper. And now it's Tuesday, and I haven't heard from him and . . ." She bit her lower lip and blinked rapidly. She didn't cry, but it looked like she came pretty close.

After a few minutes I said, "Are the weekend missions the only times Sherm is away?"

"Oh, no! Thursday nights, too. Thursdays Sherm meets his informants and passes on reports and things." Patty grimaced. "I really don't know if . . . Honestly I shouldn't be talking about Sherm's work like this. I promised. But . . ."

I was good. I shut up—a rare talent Hilda Gardner says I should display more often—and I let Patty work it out for herself. Finally she squared her shoulders and said, "No, this is the right thing to do. Sherm might need help. What else do you need to know?"

"How often and how much is Sherm paid for his, uh, intelligence activities?"

The secret agent line has been used to explain away everything from drug profits to diminished libido. Money was usually the tip-off.

Patty Akister looked at me aghast. "Pay? Sherm is a volunteer! He wouldn't take money to *serve his country*!" She actually said it that way. *Serve his country*. Poor Patty.

"Ah," I said, "I understand now."

Sherm had a girlfriend. If it had been only the Thursday nights, I'd have said he enjoyed a regular night out with the guys. Bowling, boozing, whatever. If he'd been bringing home money, I'd have added gas station holdups, or something similiar, to the list.

But if he wasn't making money at it, and he spent occasional weekends away, that meant a girlfriend. Betcha, I said to myself. No bet, I scoffed. I don't take sucker bets, especially from a sharp cookie like me.

Patty said in a timid voice, "Mr. Rafferty, can you find Sherm and help him?"

"I can find him," I said. "I need a photo, details about his day job, his exact cover story, things like that. And five hundred dollars."

Patty sighed and said, "Thank you," in a soft little voice.

"The five hundred will pay for two days work. If it looks like it will take longer than that—which I doubt—we'll talk about it. Okay?"

Patty Akister beamed. "That's fine," she said. "You have no idea how much better I feel already." She had a broad cheery face that could deliver a world-class smile, and she gave this one all she had.

I smiled back at her and meant it. I liked Patty Akister. I was a little embarrassed for her; that secret agent line was so old and so corny. And I felt sorry for her, too. Patty had a bigger problem than she thought. And paying five hundred dollars to a man like me wouldn't solve it.

Patty Akister reminded me of someone—another woman—a long time ago.

Anyway, what with all that bonhomie and compassion floating around my office, we didn't follow up on the fact that Patty had said "help" Sherm and I had said "find" Sherm.

I was pretty sure Sherm wouldn't think being found was particularly helpful.

Tough. Sherm should have thought of that before he started running the secret agent scam on my new friend Patty.

CHAPTER TWO

"This is a switch," Hilda Gardner said. "Usually you complain about people who believe outrageous lies. You call them dumb."

"Me?" I said. "Mr. Warmth and Compassion?"

"You," she said. "I recall such warm, compassionate phrases as 'bovine acceptance' and 'brains like last week's guacamole.' Well, I hate to tell you, big guy, but this Akister woman sounds a trifle dumb to me."

Hilda carefully separated one slice from the pepperoni-and-double-cheese pizza, then maneuvered that slice from the Pizza Hut box to a Limoges plate on her desk blotter. She stuck the tip of her tongue out during the cumbersome transfer. Simultaneously she melted my heart for the eight-thousandth time.

"Wrong," I said. "This isn't like last year, when I was doing security for that nutty channeler. Damn, I wonder why I did that. I must have had a severe pride deficiency that week."

"You were two months behind on your rent," Hilda said, "and too macho to take the loan I offered you."

"Ah. I do recall a certain desperation," I said. "Anyway, babe, do you remember that guy? Nineteen-year-old kid with a funny voice, claimed he turned into a Phoenician navigator or whatever it was. So there he was, supposed to be two thousand years old, zits and all, and this dork told an auditorium full of people they should go long on CDs because interest rates were going to fall. And some of them *believed* it! Now that's dumb. That's major-league dumb.'' I fiddled with the pizza slice on the antique plate on my side of Hilda's desk and tried to look aggrieved. ''Compared to that, Patty Akister is only, oh, wishful-thinking dumb. And nice dumb to boot. That's the difference.''

Beside the Limoges plates we each had a crystal champagne flute. Hilda drank chablis out of hers; I had beer. No doubt about it, lunch at Gardner's Antiques was a class act. Pizza and beer from Limoges and crystal.

Guess who brought the food and who provided the table settings.

Hilda grinned at me. ''The only difference is proximity. The people who paid to listen to that phoney were a group. Groups are remote; faceless. It was easy to be contemptuous of them. But you know this Akister woman as an individual. She's a real person to you. Then, too, it sounds like she's become another of your fallen sparrows.''

''She's a client, that's all. Woman wants her husband found; I find people. Just another job.''

Hilda reached across the desk and patted my hand. Her dark, dark eyes were large; it was one of those times when I could almost see colors in them but not quite work out what those colors were.

Hilda said, ''No, it's not just a job. And that's fine. You don't have to be one-hundred-percent rational for me to love you.''

''Does this mean you've changed your mind about a nooner?''

''You nut. I have an appointment in twenty minutes. Tell me about Patty and Sherm. How long have they been married?''

''Only six or seven months,'' I said. ''First time for each of them, Patty says.''

''Despite her age, is she as naive about men as she sounds?'' Hilda said.

''Yeah, I think so. She comes across as, oh, maybe a

small-town girl who came to the big city and got lost in a routine job for a long time. She was in training for an eventual shot at the Old Maid of the Year title, then bang! Heeerrrres . . . Shermie!''

Hilda snorted. "Some husband he is. Married six lousy months and he has a girlfriend on the side.''

"Yeah, that sucks, all right.''

Hilda said, "He's not one of those animals who con lonely spinsters, is he?''

"No. Patty doesn't have the assets to attract one of those leeches. No property. No fat bank account or insurance policy. I asked her. With all my usual tact and delicacy, of course.''

"Delicacy?'' Hilda said. "From a man who thinks haute cuisine is toasting the bread for a BLT?''

"Watch how easily I ignore that. Sherm sounds like an average guy. Nine-to-five job, three-year-old Chevy, mortgage, all that. He sells furniture at some discount place.''

"So he's not greedy,'' Hilda said. "He's still a jerk. Men!''

"He probably makes sweeping generalizations, too, the blackguard.''

"Good point.'' She frowned thoughtfully. "Are you sure he's up to something? Could there be another explanation?''

"Say, did I forget to tell you? The CIA approved my application to spy school. I'll be gone all weekend, doing basic training at this secret camp we have in Palm Springs. Don't tell anybody, okay?''

Hilda sighed. "You win.'' She looked at the rest of her pizza slice, sighed again, and put it back onto her plate. She held her glass—was it now a chablis flute?—in both hands and pushed her big desk chair back until she could prop her feet on the opened lower drawer.

"Got a nice flash of thigh that time, babe. Let me know before you go for a higher drawer.''

"Horny savage,'' she said. "So what are you going to do for Patty Akister?''

"I'm going to find Sherm.''

Hilda shook her head. "No. After that. Are you going to tell Patty where he was or not?''

I poured more beer in my glass. "I haven't worked that part out yet. It will probably come down to whatever damages her the least."

Hilda shook her head again. "Sad."

"But true. Hey, Hil, I like these flutes. They're a little bit small, but they keep the beer cold."

"A glass doesn't know what's in it," Hilda said. "Champagne or beer, the problem is the same: don't draw the cold out of the liquid, and don't let the bubbles get away." She held her flute up to the light and admired it. "These aren't true antiques, but they are pretty, aren't they?"

"Terrific. Are they expensive?" I took another sip. Nice glass. Just my speed.

Hilda smiled. "They're from a set of eight I have priced at $425."

I put the champagne flute down carefully. "No problem running them through the dishwasher, I suppose?"

CHAPTER THREE

I left Gardner's Antiques when Hilda's one-thirty appointment arrived. They were a middle-aged Turtle Creek couple who must have been married a long time. They looked more like twins than a couple. Except for the fact that she had purple hair—and more of it—I couldn't tell one from the other.

Hilda gentled them toward a richly polished dining table almost the size of Nebraska, where they chatted about patina and appreciating antique values over the next decade. Hilda had them smiling and nodding already. She's good at that sort of thing.

I slipped out the back way, dropped the empty pizza box

into a dumpster, and hit the streets. Look out, Sherm Akister, here I come.

First stop was my office on Jackson Street. It's an unusual building, a two-story tangle of small offices. It had been a radio station once, so the offices have strange floor plans and even stranger built-ins. Somewhere in there someone must have been working. Maybe. Damned if I could see it, though.

The public relations consultant was polishing the big brass letters on his door, weaving so much there was no need for wrist action to buff the metal. You may have already guessed: the PR guy drinks.

The sales manager for the door-to-door aluminum cookware place was ushering a smiling woman into his office. She had long dark hair and big hips. As he closed the door behind her, his expression made it clear there would be no sales meetings for the next hour or two.

The two women who run the secretarial service were loafing, too. So was the mail order guy. Obviously the protestant work ethic had been repealed in my absence.

When I went into my office, Beth Woodland banged on the big glass panel between my ex-radio station control room and her ex-newsroom. She and her insurance-agent boss held coffee mugs; Beth lifted half a devil's food cake off her desk. Did I want some?

No, thanks, I mimed. *Still full from lunch.* I turned my back on them, which was not easy. Beth bakes great cakes. I lied to myself about being ever-resolute in the face of temptation, grabbed the phone, and went to work.

Patty Akister hadn't tried to phone Sherm at the furniture store where he worked. Why bother? she'd said. Sherm was on a mission, not working at his day job.

Patty, Patty, Patty.

The furniture store phone rang eight times, then a man's voice said, "Yes?"

"Hi," I said. "Sherm there?"

"Who wants him?"

It was tempting to use one of the many great zingers that leapt to mind. But that wouldn't do Patty any good, so . . .

"This here's Norm Baumgartner," I said. "Been thinking

about getting me one of them La-Z-Boys. The recliner, you know? And a guy at the barber shop said I should talk to this fella Sherm. Put him on, will ya?''

After a pause the voice said, "Sherm's busy right now. Can I help you?"

"I better talk to him," I said. "I'll call back later." Sure I would.

"Okay," he said, and hung up.

That response made sense, sort of. If Sherm was off somewhere with his bimbo, it figured he would have his buddies cover for him. But it was funny that the guy didn't push harder to sell me a La-Z-Boy. Maybe the discount furniture sales game isn't as hardball as I thought. Or maybe he guessed I wanted Sherm for the wrong reasons; maybe Sherm got calls from bill collectors all the time. Maybe.

Next I phoned the cop shop. "Durkee," Ed growled.

"Lieutenant Deadeye Durkee?" I said. "This is *People* magazine. May I interview you for a feature article on fearless, straight-shooting lawmen who wear brown suits?"

"Knock it off, Rafferty," Ed said. "What do you want this time?"

"Depends on how we stand at the moment, Ed. Do you owe me, do I owe you, or are we about even?"

"I hate to admit it, but I owe you," he said. "Not much, though, so watch it." Ed's voice became slightly hollow; I could imagine him holding the phone with his shoulder while he pawed through the piles of paperwork on his desk, looking for something he wouldn't be able to find.

"Sherman Gaines Akister," I said. I read Akister's address and his Chevy's license number out of my notebook. "I don't think you'll have anything on this guy, Ed. But check anyway, will you?"

"Why?"

"It looks like Sherm is shacked up somewhere with a girlfriend. His wife wants me to find him. So if he has any record with you—which I doubt—it might point me in the right direction. I'm just covering all the bases, like it says here on page twelve of *So You Want To Be A Famous Private Detective*."

"Okay."

"Boy, you never let a guy get a word in edgewise, do you?" But Ed was gone by then, so I hung up, too.

Finally I called Akister's home. Patty answered. "It's Rafferty," I said. "Sherm hasn't shown up, has he?"

"No," Patty said. Her voice was small and lonely. It would have been tough for her, going back to that empty house. I felt sorry for her all over again. You don't have to be a genius to get hurt.

"Cheer up," I said, "I'm going to find him. Is it okay if I come over there and have a look around?"

"Well . . ."

"I don't want to pry, Mrs. Akister, but—"

"Call me Patty. Please."

"All right. Patty. The thing is, Sherm might have inadvertently left a clue to where he went on his mission." I was getting better; I said "his mission" without stumbling.

Patty said, "Oh, I doubt it. Sherm is very careful."

"I'm sure he is, but . . ."

After a longish pause, she said, "Well, maybe you're right. After all, you're a trained investigator."

I winched. When she said "trained investigator" it sounded too much like "secret agent" and "on a mission."

"I'll be there in about fifteen minutes," I said. "And if Sherm has any, ah, espionage material or equipment you know of, I want to see it." She drew a breath, so I hurried on. "I'm treating all this as classified, Patty. Strictly confidential."

"All right." She hung up gently without saying good-bye.

On the way out of the building, as I passed the cookware office again, the door flew open and the dark-haired woman stormed out. Her cheeks were bright and her eyes angry. She pushed around me and stalked away. Her back was very straight, and her heels clacked loudly in the narrow corridor.

The sales manager sauntered into the open doorway, relighting half a cigar. He glanced at her retreating back and shrugged. "Women," he said to me between puffs. "Who can figure 'em?"

"Who indeed?" I said.

* * *

The Akisters lived in east Dallas. Close-in east, between downtown and Buckner Park. Their house was small and neat. So was their neighborhood. Small, neat, and getting smaller; squeezed between the yuppie playpens on lower Greenville Avenue and the gentrification of Deep Ellum. Some people call it progress.

Patty Akister answered her doorbell before it finished bonging. Her cheeks were pale, and her fingers trembled as she shoved a book-shaped box into my hands. "Look," she said. "It's empty."

Well, not quite. The box wasn't completely empty. It still had a blank warranty card in it, and a small brochure, and one oily pull-through cleaning patch. The Browning logo was printed on the lid and repeated inside, near the gun-shaped depression where the BDA .380 pistol had rested.

Patty's voice was shaky. "I . . . I never knew he had a gun." She reached out to touch the box. Gingerly she put her fingers into the place where the pistol wasn't. "He must have taken it with him. On his mission."

She looked up at me and her large blue eyes welled with tears. "Now I'm really worried, Mr. Rafferty."

CHAPTER FOUR

"A gun," Patty Akister said for the thirty-ninth time. "It scares me, to think of Sherm having a gun."

Patty and I sat at opposite ends of her kitchen table. There was a checked tablecloth on the table, and a small bowl of flowers, and coffee cups. And a plate of what may have been the best baking-powder biscuits of the century. The two biscuits I'd already eaten were that good, anyway. I buttered a third, just to make sure.

"What if Sherm gets shot?" Patty said. There was a little catch in her voice.

"He won't get shot."

Patty couldn't seem to take her eyes off the empty Browning box. There was a gunshop price sticker on the box lid. $352.85, it said, which sounded about right. Good handguns don't come cheap. I peeled the sticker off the box.

"Does that tell you anything?" Patty said.

"I don't know yet." I pressed the sticker onto a page in my pocket notebook and jotted down the pistol's serial number from the warranty card. Then I put the box on the seat of the chair next to me and shoved it out of sight under the table.

Patty sighed and pushed the plate of biscuits toward me. "Sherm loves fresh-baked biscuits. I fixed these when I got home because that made it seem like . . ." She sniffed and blinked. "Have another one, please."

"Well . . ." I took my fourth biscuit and told myself it was only to make Patty feel better. Sure it was.

"Mr. Rafferty, do you think Sherm's all right?"

"He's all right," I said.

"But the gun . . . ?"

Actually that bothered me, too. The pistol just didn't fit. Oh, there are a few would-be Rambos who invent espionage fairy tales for the boys at the local bar, but generally phoney secret agents aren't gun toters. They're plotters and talkers, not doers. A fairly high percentage of them are salesmen.

Yes, I know that's a generalization based on an absurdly small sample and subject to error. So what? When the TV networks stop, so will I.

But the immediate problem was Patty. She imagined her fearless hero Sherm in a back alley, swapping hot lead with fiendish KGB goons. That was bad enough; it would be worse to tell her he was probably in a no-tell motel, doing the Posturepedic foxtrot with his girlfriend. I chewed on Patty's problem and her baking-powder biscuit simultaneously.

Finally I said, "The gun doesn't necessarily mean he's getting shot at. Or that he's shooting at anyone else. Maybe it's not his gun. Maybe he's returning it to the owner. Or maybe he's had it for years. Maybe he forgot about it, found

it recently, and took it away to sell so it didn't frighten you."
I showed her one of my better smiles. I was going for comforting on that smile, with just a trace of big-brother-will-fix-it.

"Then why didn't he take the box?" Patty said.

"Great biscuits," I said. "I'm going to work now. How long have you lived in this house?"

Patty frowned at the change of pace. "Not very long," she said. "When we got married, I gave up my apartment and moved here."

"I should have said: how long has Sherm lived here?"

"Oh, now let me think. He said he bought it quite a while ago as a rent house. You know, as an investment. But after several years he began to have problems with tenants. He had to spend a lot of money fixing the house up again, so he moved in. . . . Oh, darn, four years ago? Five? I can't remember exactly."

"That's close enough." I stood up. "I can't explain very well what I do, but if I can get a feeling for Sherm, that will help me find him. I'd like to wander around the house now. Is that a problem for you?"

"Nooo, I guess not, but . . . I could show you around."

"It's better if you don't. I'll ask if I need help."

"Well, all right."

I left her sitting in the kitchen—I'd seen enough to know that was Patty's space, not Sherm's—and went into the living room. Twenty seconds later Patty bustled in.

"One thing," she said. "That box the gun came in. I found it in the garage, under Sherm's workbench."

"Thank you," I said.

We looked at each other for a minute, then Patty nodded and went back into the kitchen. I went snooping, just ambling at first, drifting from room to room, soaking up impressions.

It's a specialized kind of voyeurism, that process of exploring the unguarded places where people live, then constructing an image of them. Depending on the place and the people—and my mood—it can be almost addictive. I understand what motivates archeologists. And some burglars, too, I bet.

The Akisters' furniture was mid-range in price and quality. Some of it was new; the bedroom suite and an armchair in the living room, for example. I decided those pieces had been bought when they married. There were a few items that Patty had obviously brought with her. At least I didn't think Sherm had a sewing table and a hope chest during his bachelor days.

The rest of the blandly masculine furniture was worn, but not worn out. It looked comfortable. I know about worn and comfortable. My furniture looks like that.

The house was spotlessly clean. I credited Patty with the final gloss, but the general condition said Sherm had been a neat bachelor.

I realized that was the second time I had automatically slotted Sherm and Patty into *Happy Days* gender roles. Still, it felt right for them. Patty certainly acted that way; the house and furnishings fit, too. And Sherm's secret agent routine dated back to the cold war.

In the living room, two armchairs faced a good-sized television set. There was a table beside each chair and a floor lamp between them. Sherm's chair was a brown recliner; Patty used a floral-patterned rocker. There was embroidery equipment in a bag beside the rocker. A fat Ludlum novel on Sherm's table had a page dog-eared near the middle. Behind the chairs, against the wall, there was a fair-sized bookshelf three-quarters filled with Reader's Digest Condensed Book volumes. There were knickknacks in the gaps.

Except for a VCR under the television set, the Akisters didn't have many gadgets. There was no computer, maybe because there were no kids in the house. But there was no pool, spa, wet bar, or billiard table, either. And I hadn't noticed a food processor, pasta maker, or bread-baking whatzit in the kitchen, either.

Enough sociology. It was time for Rafferty's Rule Seventeen: People lie, appearances lie, bank accounts never lie. Well, hardly ever.

Sherm apparently used one of the spare bedrooms as a study. He had an old blond desk in there, and he filed things by the drawer system. The "banking" drawer was the most organized, probably because it was used most often. Sherm's bank statements showed weekly deposits between $350 and $450. Those would be his paychecks, I decided, changing from week to week with his sales commissions. So, what with withholding and Social Security and such, Sherm probably earned about twenty-five thousand a year, give or take.

Last year's 1040 confirmed that. $26,582 gross.

There was a savings account, too, with almost eighteen thousand dollars in it. That was a little more than I expected, but some of it might have been Patty's savings. And, besides, Sherm had been supporting only himself until recently.

I found a savings-and-loan statement in what seemed to be Sherm's "house" drawer. Dallas real estate was down now, but it had boomed several times since Sherm bought that house. It showed. His mortgage payments were a lot less than I paid in rent. No wonder he could save money.

There was also a bookshelf in Sherm's study. In here almost all the books were paperbacks, some of them pretty old. He had a worn copy of *The Ipcress File*, for example, with a cover price you wouldn't believe, and two or three other early Deighton books I recognized. The paperbacks were almost all spy novels or had, at least, international adventure themes.

There will be no extra points awarded for guessing where Sherm got the idea to become a "secret agent."

In the garage Sherm's workbench wasn't much. He was definitely not a do-it-yourselfer. He had a few tools in a green plastic toolbox, a shelf with old paint cans on it, and eight glass jars filled with rusty screws and nails. There was a lawn mower in one corner, a shovel and rake in another, and a scattering of the usual junk everyone has cluttering up their garage.

I found a gap behind the paint cans where I thought the gun box had been, then confirmed it by finding the ammunition eight inches away.

It was a box of fifty 9-mm shorts. They'd fit a .380 chamber, and there were exactly twenty-six of them missing. Twenty-six shells is two full clips for a BDA. I didn't like that very much. Every time I thought I had Sherm figured, the pistol problem cropped up.

Forty-five minutes after I'd started, I was back in the Akisters' living room, trying to put it all together. I sat in Sherm's chair and thought.

Ordinary. That was the major impression. Sherm seemed to be an ordinary guy, living an ordinary life. He had a new wife who would do anything for him, the bastard, but he'd conned her with the corniest line in town, then stepped out with some bimbo.

And he took an automatic pistol with him.

I vaguely remembered reading somewhere that spies, real spies, typically adopt a bland persona. What if Sherm really . . .

C'mon, Rafferty! Next thing, you'll be buying gold bricks or New Age crystals.

Patty came tentatively out of the kitchen then and offered me another biscuit.

"I forgot to tell you before," she said, "but I have a jar of honey, if you like honey on your biscuits."

"There are things I like more than honey on fresh biscuits," I said. "but offhand I can't think of any."

"Oh, good," Patty said. "And I made a fresh pot of coffee, too."

So I ate the biscuit with honey and loved it. The one after that was pretty good, too. And while I ate, Patty talked.

"I know you think I'm silly," she said, "but I honestly don't know what I'd do if anything happened to Sherm."

"Not silly," I said, though it may have been a trifle muffled by the biscuit.

Patty leaned on the table and looked at me. "I was an old maid, Mr. Rafferty. Thirty-six isn't old, I know, but I was an old maid. I was the one who was always there to take up the office collections and remember everyone else's birthday and offer to work late, because there was no one waiting for me at home. I hadn't dated since the high-school prom. And I didn't get asked to the prom until the last day.

"My sisters got married early," she said. "Both of them. Their houses are full of children and laughter and . . . I was Aunt Patty; the odd one out. That's why I left Buffalo. A new start, I thought. But that was three years ago, and I was about to give up." She looked a me quizzically. "Do you have any idea how hard it is to meet men? Well, for a woman like me to meet men? I even—I can't believe I did it—I even tried one of those computer dating places. It was horrible; I've never been so embarrassed in my entire life."

Patty blinked. There was hurt in her eyes and fear, too. "Those were terrible days. Terrible. And then I met Sherm. I went to buy a coffee table, and I found a husband. I always thought those things only happened in the movies, but . . . Sherm changed my life, Mr. Rafferty. He loves me, and he lets me love him, and I've never been so happy in my life. It took too long for that to happen; it can't stop so soon."

She carefully shifted the butter dish two inches to the right. "When I gave notice at the office, some of the girls said I was silly to quit. Estelle especially. I think she's a feminist. She reads all those books, anyway. Estelle thought it was terrible that I was going to stop working and be a housewife. Just a housewife, she called it."

Patty smiled. "If only she knew how long I'd wanted to be a housewife. I love being here when Sherm comes home from work; I like to cook and clean and keep things nice. What can be wrong with that? I know people laugh at that attitude these days, but . . ."

Patty reached out to grab my arm. "We're just plain people. Sherm and I aren't grabbers; we don't hurt people. We're happy with each other and with what we have. You have to find him, Mr. Rafferty, and help him. You have to!" She looked down at her hand as if it belonged to someone else. "I'm sorry." She dropped her hands into her lap and put her head down. Her shoulders moved slowly as she wept.

As she sobbed, I felt useless and angry. Angry at Sherm and his unknown girlfriend for deluding this poor woman and angry at myself because I didn't know how to fix the mess he'd created.

And angry, too, because I couldn't think of any reasons why Sherm left for his "mission" with a loaded pistol.

No, that's not true. I could think of reasons; I just couldn't think of any reason I wanted to explain later to Patty Akister.

CHAPTER FIVE

"He's *what*?" I said into the telephone.

"Akister is connected," Ed Durkee said. "He's a bagman for some mob minor-leaguer named . . . ah, damn, I got it here somewhere . . . Manny something, anyway."

"Sherm Akister?" I said. "A bagman?" Ed's call had awakened me. I fumbled for my watch. Surprise. It wasn't very early, not nearly as early as it felt. Beside me Hilda stirred and mumbled and burrowed deeper under the covers.

"Bagman," Ed said. He sounded like he'd had a full eight hours, a good breakfast, and was enjoying his day. "I got a hefty file here on your buddy Akister—"

"Did you sprinkle anything unusual over your corn flakes this morning?"

"—and you have a ten-thirty appointment with a sergeant from the Intelligence Unit. The IU guys wonder why, all of sudden, you pop up looking for one of the no-goods on their list. My office. Up and at 'em tiger."

"What's this all ab—"

"Ten-thirty," Ed said. "Be here." He hung up without breaking into laughter, but I had the impression it had been a close call.

I got up then and stood by the window, scratching and stretching and yawning. Outside Cat jumped the back fence and padded toward the house.

In the bed behind me, Hilda stirred again. "Wazzatime?" she said muzzily.

I told her. She groaned something that may or may not have been, "Twenty minutes."

"You got it," I said, and went to make coffee.

While the coffee perked, I let Cat in and splashed milk into a saucer for him. He hadn't been around for a few days; doubtless the heavy pressure of feline business. Looked like it from the fresh scratch over his left eye, anyway.

Cat really belonged to the woman who lived behind me. At least, that's what she claimed. But then she called him Muffin, for God's sake, and she had four dozen plastic curlers permanently implanted in her hair. No wonder Cat spent so much time at my house.

When I carried two cups of coffee back to the bedroom, Hilda was still asleep. In the time it took me to put a cup on her beside table, walk around to my side, get in, and pick up my cup again, she was awake. She was sitting up, sipping coffee, and smiling.

I don't know how she does that.

Hilda said, "Did we really stay up until two-thirty watching an old Bogart movie?"

"And eating popcorn. Don't forget the popcorn. Besides, *Treasure of the Sierra Madre* is not just 'an old movie,' Hil. Have a little respect."

"Well . . ."

"An insightful film reviewer would call it a thought-provoking study of avarice and pressure; a masterpiece of characterization."

"Ho, ho. You only wanted to see the routine about the badges again. 'I don't have a badge,' or whatever it is."

"That is a base canard," I said. "Unworthy of you."

"Uh-huh. What was the phone call?"

I told her.

"Weird," she said. "He doesn't sound like a mafioso. I mean, I don't know what a mafioso is like, exactly, but whatever it is, Akister's not one of them. Am I making any sense?"

"You are to me. Maybe the cops screwed it up. Maybe there's another Akister who's the hood." I finished my coffee and got out of bed again. "I guess I'll find out at this heavy-duty meeting Ed set up."

Hilda got out of bed, too, and stood on her side, looking at me with a half smile on her face. "How will you get into police headquarters, big guy? Won't you have to show them a badge?"

"Bodge?" I said indignantly. "Bodge? I don't got to show them no steenking bodge!"

"That's it," Hilda said. "Almost perfect. Now Bogart shoots you, doesn't he?"

"Cut," I said, with too much dignity, because she darted away and beat me to the shower by a full step and a half.

"You'll pay for dat one, schweetheart," I yelled over the suddenly drumming shower.

Hilda stuck her head, and her tongue, out at me.

I reached in past her and twisted the cold water on all the way. She shrieked and jumped out, wet and slippery, digging her fingers into my side, trying to tickle me. She keeps doing that, which is silly because I'm not ticklish, but she is. So I tickled her.

And what with the tickling, and one thing and another, she was late getting to her office, and I barely made my ten-thirty appointment with Ed Durkee and the Dallas Police Intelligence Unit genius who knew all about Sherm Akister.

CHAPTER SIX

Ralph Mancuso was tired. Very tired. Or maybe he always looked like that. After a few minutes I decided Mancuso's appearance of bone-weariness came from his soft spaniel eyes. Those, and the way he slumped in his chair and spoke very slowly and very softly, like he was about to fall asleep at any moment.

"Akister is not a heavy dude," Mancuso said. "Far from it. Neither is his boss, particularly, depending on how you measure it. But something's stirring in that organization, and we don't know what it is. Trouble for someone, I'd say. Which usually means us, in the long run." Saying all that took a long time.

Mancuso had a shaggy, red-brown beard and long hair. Long by DPD standards, anyway. He wore a brown leather bomber jacket and wheat-colored slacks and scuffed beige Hush Puppies. He was thirty, maybe thirty-two, but he could have passed for younger if he'd been more animated.

I said, "Exactly how 'not heavy' are Akister and his boss? I figure good old Sherm to be halfway pissed-off when I find him and his girlfriend. Is that going to be poke-in-the-eye pissed-off or concrete-overshoes-in-the-Trinity-River pissed-off?"

Mancuso swiveled his head around to face me—slowly, what else?—and arched his eyebrows. "It's hard to say. We had Hinkston—that's Akister's boss, Manny Hinkston—we had Hinkston figured for poke-in-the-eye until three months ago. Since then he's been working his way up into the concrete-overshoes category. Of course, that's Hinkston, not Akister."

Then, after he'd thought about it for a minute, Mancuso added, "Thing is, guys like Hinkston look after their people, so who knows for sure?"

Behind his desk, Ed Durkee nodded to himself. In the third visitor's chair, Sergeant Ricco fidgeted with the buttons on his snappy sports jacket. Ricco was short and skinny, with a look of rat-cunning on his face. He had been quiet for almost five minutes now, and he was getting twitchy. Sitting and listening, especially listening to a slow talker like Mancuso, was obviously tough for Ricco. He liked to be on the street, watching, hustling, scheming. If Ricco had been around in the twenties, Damon Runyon wouldn't have had to invent him.

Finally Ricco said, "Give me a break, Ed. I've been up all night listening to a cranked-up weasel claim he didn't cut an eighty-two-year-old great-grandmother. Today's my day off, but who'd know it? Again. So can we quit fucking around here and get to the point? You got the file, Ed. Read it. Mancuso knows all this shit by heart but it's gonna take him twelve goddamn years to tell us.''

Mancuso nodded like he was keeping time with a dirge. He'd probably heard that complaint before.

Ed shrugged. "Okay. For Ricco and Rafferty, here's the background.'' Ed looked up from the file and said to Mancuso, "If I leave anything out, say so.''

Ed was head down and leafing through the file before Mancuso said, "Okay.''

"Manny Hinkston,'' Ed said, "aka Manny Hink, Marty Hinkley, and Manny Stone. Hinkston came to Dallas from Kansas City, ah, almost twenty years ago. According to this, the locals made a place for him. Why was that, Ralph?''

Mancuso whipped into action. It was only six or eight seconds before the first word came out. "That was after the top family reallocated the Kansas City territory. Hinkston was working for a hood named Jerry Giacollato then. Jerry the G. We don't know why, exactly, but Giacollato got taken out. A restaurant job. A classic. Antipasto, clams marinara, and boom, boom, boom. The story is that Hinkston fingered his boss for that hit. He had to leave KC then, but the crowd that took over Jerry the G's action worked it out so Hinkston got a small slice of the action here.''

"How small?'' I said.

"Pretty small,'' Ed said, taking a single sheet out of the file. "At the moment, he's doing a little shylocking, plus he owns a hot-car garage, and two, maybe three, whorehouses.''

"Three,'' Mancuso said. "We finally tied the third one to him day before yesterday. The paperwork'll catch up.''

"My, my,'' I said. "All that sin and degradation. What are decent folks to think?''

Mancuso sniffed. "I said he was small-time. Take his shylocking business. As far as we can tell, Manny has less than a hundred thou on the street at any one time. The car-boosting gig is penny-ante, too; five or six units a week busted down for parts. About the same with the girls. Hinkston puts two or three hookers into an apartment, pays their fines if we bust them, and then finds a new place if we crowd them or the neighbors complain too much.''

Ed said, ''That's where Akister fits in, Rafferty. Every Thursday he collects the house cut from the girls and takes it back to Hinkston.''

''Bullshit,'' Ricco said. ''This lame-o only picks up his cut once a week? No way!''

Mancuso nodded ponderously. ''Of course not. He takes his cut every night, just like every other pimp. But *Akister* only picks up the money on Thursday nights, because that's the regular guy's day off.''

I asked if Hinkston's hoods had pension plans and personalized parking spaces, but they all ignored me. So I told them about Sherm's Thursday night spycraft and his periodic weekend ''missions.''

''That fits,'' Mancuso said. ''Every once in a while, Manny gets Akister to drive wetbacks up to Kansas City.''

Ed pawed through the file with a frown on his face.

''Relax, Ed, it's not in there,'' Mancuso said. ''I should have said, we *think* that's what happening. There's talk in KC about a vanload of wetbacks arriving there every third or fourth weekend. Down at the border end, the INS guys hear talk of a coyote run, with a Dallas changeover point and a Kansas City or Chicago final destination. Plus, we know Akister has flown back into town—from KC—on at least six weekends this year. So it makes sense.'' He shrugged. ''That one is Immigration's problem, really. We're only coordinating on it.''

''I'll be damned,'' I said. ''I thought he had a girlfriend.''

Ed said, ''Not such a bad guess. His moves figure either way.''

Mancuso said, ''As far as we know, Akister is very low-level. Just a wage slave doing his job. Most of the time he sells furniture. Hinkston uses an el cheapo furniture operation as a front.''

During Mancuso's standard five second pause between sentences, Ed cut in with, ''Hinkston Bargain Furniture, on Garland Road.''

"But sometimes," Mancuso went on, "Manny needs an extra man on the shifty side, so he uses Sherm. We think that's because Sherm is a fairly pliable guy."

Ricco looked at Mancuso suspiciously. "Gimme ten minutes, I can show you four bad-asses running stronger, crookeder operations than this Hinkston scuzz. Why are you IU hotshots so interested in him?"

"Well, that's the whole point," Mancuso said at half speed. "That's what I've been telling you. Manny Hinkston's operation is changing. There's the wetback operation, for one thing. That's new. The worst part, though, is he's getting tougher. Meaner. Manny leans on people now, like he wants blood as much as the money. The word is out on the street: You get your arm broken the first day you're late with the vig on a Hinkston loan."

Ricco sneered. "Shylocks always break arms."

Mancuso shook his head. "Not as quick as Hinkston does. Not now. He's letting some of his hookers roll johns, too, and before long someone will get hurt there. Hell, he's even coming down hard on the girls. Most of Manny's stables are pretty clean. For pros, at least. But he's treating them like streetcorner scag hags. If they don't turn enough tricks to suit him, they get hurt. They won't tell us that, of course. We're not likely to get that lucky. But that's what the street says."

"Old news," Ricco said. "Those guys always whale the shit out of their girls. Tell me something I don't know."

"All right," Mancuso said, "I will. Hinkston's torching his competition. We can't prove that, of course. No one will admit their pile of hot ashes used to be a whorehouse, or claim Hinkston did it, so there's no evidentiary support. But I'm pretty damned sure of three firebombings, and I suspect two more. They're all in the turf surrounding Hinkston's territory. I think he wants to expand the easy way."

Ed frowned. Ed did great frowns. His malleable face collapsed and wrinkled to match his rumpled suit. "There'll be hell to pay if those guys start a running war on the street."

Mancuso nodded. "Right. And that's why I jumped when Records said you were checking on Akister. Now I know it's Rafferty here and the wife who really want to find Sherm, but that's okay. Whatever the angle is, I'll work it, as long as it helps me find out what Hinkston is up to." After a long pause, Mancuso added, "And stop him."

I said, "I wonder where Sherm Akister is. Apparently he's not shagging a girlfriend, so why isn't he at home? Or is he still away on a wetback run?"

Mancuso shook his head. "I checked on that. Akister flew back into Dallas/Fort Worth Sunday afternoon. That was three days ago. We don't know where he is now, but mostly that's because we haven't looked for him. My boss okayed a surveillance of Hinkston's furniture place after I talked to Ed late yesterday."

Mancuso checked his watch. "They'll be in place by now, so we'll know something today, I hope. If Akister showed up for work today, well, that's one thing. But if Akister's gone to ground, Christ only knows what nasty little chore Hinkston gave him this time."

"He's carrying now," I said. "Did you know that?"

"Goddamn," Mancuso said. "That's not like our boy Sherm."

I told them about the Browning and gave Ed the gunshop sticker and serial number. Mancuso said, "Goddamn," again. He seemed pretty upset.

I said, "Let's not forget here, I'm working for his wife. I want to let her down easy."

Mancuso said, "We can do that. No problem. I'm pretty sure she's clean, and the way I hear it, Sherm is totally apeshit about her. I'd bet that "spy" line was his way of not telling her what he really does for Hinkston." Mancuso's beard split open in a wide grin. "So how about you swoop down on old Sherm and tell him the jig is up. Tell him you'll tell the wife unless he cooperates. Then you can introduce him to all your friends down here on the city payroll."

"Sounds reasonable," I said. "I'll have to find him first, though."

Mancuso's grin hadn't budged. "Sherm's due for his bagman gig tomorrow night. I'll show you where."

"Unless the schedule's been changed," Ed said. "Or, like

you said, unless Manny's moved Sherm on to bigger and better things.''

Then Mancuso's grin went away. "I hope not," he said ponderously, "or we're in deep shit.''

CHAPTER SEVEN

Mancuso left Ed's office at the same speed he did everything else. Ed, Ricco, and I watched him go. And watched and watched.

When Mancuso was finally gone, Ricco said, "Goddamn. He makes a snail look like it's on fast forward, don't he?''

Ed dry-washed his rubbery face and yawned. "Ingram, over in the IU, says they all call him Sleepy. No wonder.''

I said, "What's the story with whorehouses at the moment, Ed?''

Ricco chirped up with, "They're fulla broads. Money changes hands, then they—''

"Oh, I wouldn't charge them anything. At least, not if they said thank you afterwards.''

"Oh, for Christ's sake," Ed said. "Will you two knock if off?'' He rubbed his face again and shook his head. "Sleepy, is right! I'm about to . . .'' After another yawn he said, "Okay, what you want to know is what you'll be walking into tomorrow night, right?''

"Right.''

"I don't know," Ed said, picking up his phone. "But Art Sigwhit probably does.''

Art Sigwhit was a vice cop. He was short, wiry, black, and he knew everything there was to know about prostitution in Dallas.

"Okay," he said, "first you got your down-and-dirty street girls. Lots of them underage, most of them junkies. Some of them work car jobs, sometimes they got a room set up close by. South Dallas, west Dallas, places like that."

"A step or two up from there," I said.

"Okay. Little bit up from that—not much sometimes—you got your hitchhikers. They work the major roads. Central Expressway, Northwest, Harry Hines, places like that. I busted one on Mockingbird Lane night before last."

"Hitchhiking hookers?" I said.

"Oh, yeah. Man on his own picks them up, and he'll be lucky to get up to the speed limit before she offers to blow him for fifty bucks, something like that. There's some tough chickies hitchhiking. They have to be; they take a lot of chances."

"They're not the only ones."

Sigwhit lighted a cigarette and screwed his right eye up to avoid the smoke. "Put it this way. If they made titanium rubbers, I wouldn't screw one of those broads."

"Nice imagery," I said. "Another step up."

"Okay. Next up, but again not real far, would be some of those 'nude modeling' studios, especially the real scummy ones in the industrial districts. I don't know why guys go to those joints. I hate to even walk in the door, and I've got a legit reason to be there. And I've got a gun."

"But do the galloping staphylococci know that?"

Sigwhit cantered his head and pointed his finger at me. "Right! Anyway, from there up, you're getting into your typical middle-class American whorehouse. They call themselves modeling studios or escort agencies or massage parlors. Look in the phone book. Half the time they call themselves all three. Whatever, they're just a place to go get laid. Or the girls will come to you, but I guess that's not what you're interested in."

I said, "No. I want to know about how they set up in apartments. Do they arrange for security? Any heavies hanging around? That sort of thing."

Art Sigwhit ground out his cigarette and shrugged. "It depends. Some parts of town there are more bouncers than whores. On the other hand, at the top end of the market, your grand-a-night snuggle-bunny doesn't need muscle. She's screwing guys who show her off in fancy restaurants. She's not too worried about running into kinks.''

"How about the middle of the road?'' I said. I dug out the addresses Mancuso had given me and showed them to Sigwhit.

He pointed to the second address. "This is Manny Hinkston's setup, right?''

"They all are. Supposed to be, anyway.''

"Ed says you're going to lift a bagman out of one of these places.''

"Then it must be so.''

"Hmmm.'' Sigwhit frowned at the paper. "You'll probably find these are two- or three-bedroom apartments. One of the hookers might live there. Don't expect to see signs of anything like that; some of the neighbors won't even know what's going on. The business will be coming from raunchy newspaper ads and word-of-mouth. Normally I'd say there wouldn't be anyone there but the girls, but Hinkston's getting flaky lately. You might find a hardass hanging around, keeping an eye on the operation. Or traveling with the bagman, backing him up.'' He shrugged again. "It's hard to say. You'll have to deal with what you find.''

"When you put undercover men in to bust these places, how do they get in?''

"Sometimes they call first and set up a time like your typical john. Sometimes they show up and talk their way in. Waving money around usually helps.''

"Any other hints?''

Sigwhit chewed his lip briefly. "Whether you run up against in-house muscle or not, be careful. If one of the girls has a customer with her, things might turn squirrelly. You wouldn't believe how crazy your average Sunday-school teacher can get when you catch him porking a hooker. They go berserk sometimes. Watch yourself.''

"Never fear,'' I said. "My heart is pure and my strength is as of ten.''

Sigwhit grinned up at me. "And you're crazy as hell, too. That should help."

CHAPTER EIGHT

Hilda and I went to a movie that night. *Rain Man.* We'd missed it the first time around, and Hilda wanted to see it. So did a lot of other people. The line was pretty long.

"I hope you like this," Hilda said, hugging my arm and shivering a little. It was cool that evening and breezy. The radio said showers later.

I said, "It has to be better than that dog of a video you rented last week."

"You really hated *Broadcast News*, didn't you?"

"Damn right. Who wants to watch a movie about losers? I can't believe I wasted an hour and a half watching three emotional cripples never do anything right."

"It didn't have any shooting, either," Hilda said. "Or fistfights or car chases."

We made it to the head of the line then. I gave the ticket seller a twenty and said, "This isn't a movie about losers, is it?" Hilda poked me in the side.

The woman behind the glass panel shoved out two tickets, my change, and said, "You'll love it."

"Car chases? Gunfights?" I said. Hilda poked me again.

"You'll love it," the ticket seller repeated. "Hoffman is superb. Next!"

Inside, we had to wait in the lobby until they'd finished the previous showing. I got a bucket of popcorn, double butter. We stood in the middle of the herd and nibbled.

Hilda said softly, "This man Patty Akister's husband

works for. Hinkston? What kind of name is that for a mafia boss?''

''Some mafia boss,'' I said. ''They let him run a little action on the side, that's all. Trouble is, he wants to expand.''

A chunky guy in baggy pants and a yellow jacket stood ten feet behind Hilda. He was eyeing her backside and legs. I stared at him; he looked away.

''Expansion is a logical business move,'' Hilda said. ''But eventually there must be a practical limit to the available market. So what's the prostitution industry's version of an unfriendly takeover?'' She ate three or four kernels of popcorn and licked butter off her fingertips.

Big Eyes in the tracksuit top was back facing this way again, staring at Hilda's rear end. I said to Hilda, ''A firebomb through the front door. Broken legs. A .22 slug behind the ear. Depends on how unfriendly the takeover is.''

''Gross,'' she said.

''Speaking of gross . . .'' Big Eyes was shuffling closer to Hilda. He had one hand in his pants pocket and the other dangling oh-so-casually at his side. He didn't try to disguise his interest.

I reached out past Hilda and snapped my fingers to get his attention. He stopped abruptly, three or four feet away. ''Unauthorized leching in a public place,'' I said. ''It's a proven health hazard.''

He tried a weak ''who, me?'' look, but then he seemed to realize how quiet the lobby had become. He looked around, saw people staring at us, and decided to go stand somewhere else.

''I wish you wouldn't do that,'' Hilda said. ''He wasn't causing any trouble.''

''He was about to,'' I said. ''Consider yourself saved from the phantom clutcher.''

''Oh.'' Hilda looked over her shoulder. People around us turned back into their own groups and restarted their conversations. The crowd buzz slowly grew again.

Hilda twitched a hesitant smile and said, ''Thank you, I

guess. I just get embarrassed when I think you're going to start a fight.''

"You'll know if I'm going to fight. I'll let you hold the popcorn."

Someone opened a set of double doors, and people started to flow out of the theater. When they had finished, we flowed in and found seats. I didn't see Big Eyes sitting anywhere near us.

"The thing is, babe, it's bad for everybody when the different small mobs don't go along with the generally accepted territories.''

"Everybody?"

"Almost. Civilians can get caught up in the fighting. The bad guys lose business because of public attention. And the police time and paperwork involved is incredible. Plus, when the territorial war is over, the cops have to start from scratch again. Now who's doing what and why and to whom? It's not easy being a cop now," I said. "Glad I gave it up when I did.''

Hilda reached for more popcorn. Good thing I'd bought the giant-size bucket. "Tell me this," she said. "Why don't the police find Sherm Akister, instead of letting you do it?"

" 'Cause they're playing the angles," I said. "Suppose they staked out the neighborhood climax-orama and picked up Sherm with his pockets full of money. Sherm would say he only stopped to ask which way to the bowling alley, the money is a deposit on a dining room set he sold them, and by the way, where's his lawyer?''

"Seriously . . ."

"Count on it. Or Sherm might clam up. Whichever, he'd be bailed out before you could say police frustration.''

"What about the prostitutes?"

" 'These women, your honor?' Sherm's lawyer would say. 'These women sitting around in their underwear? Merely a Madonna look-alike contest. Motion to dismiss.' '' I chewed on a handful of popcorn, then said, "Knowing something is easy, Hil. Proving it in court is the hard part.''

Hilda said, "That's just too bad. That's the police department's job. It's not fair for them to use you.''

"It makes sense, though. I want to find Sherm and get him home to Patty. If a few well-chosen threats will turn him into a police snitch at the same time, then, hey, Mancuso is ahead of the game. If I bomb out, he hasn't lost anything. It's a good move on his part."

"Will Sherm show up tomorrow night?"

"Probably. I got a call from Mancuso this afternoon. Sherm went to work at the furniture place today."

"Why isn't he going home?" Hilda said.

"Beats me. Mancuso's guys are going to tail him tonight, see where he's holing up."

Hilda put her hand on my arm. "Are you—"

The lights dimmed and the movie started. "Watch this," I said. "I hear Hoffman is superb."

CHAPTER NINE

The phone was ringing when I unlocked the office door the next morning. It was Patty Akister.

"Oh, Mr. Rafferty, I thought I'd missed you. I was about to hang up."

We listened to each other breathe for a moment, then Patty said, "I'm sorry to bother you, but, ah, have you, ah, learned anything yet? I just thought . . ."

Patty sounded as innocent and needing as a hungry cocker spaniel. I worked up my most reassuring voice for her. "Things are going well, Patty. Good news soon, I hope. Tomorrow, maybe."

"Oh that's wonderful. Could you, ah, tell me what . . . ?"

More reassuring tones. "I'm afraid it's not possible for me to discuss a case in progress, but, um, things are definitely looking up." Be gentle, Rafferty. Don't let her sit home and worry about Sherm.

"That's good," Patty said. "Only, I'd hoped . . . Well, I'll hear from you tomorrow, is that right?"

"Yes, I'll call you. Try to relax now, Patty. Everything will be all right." I sounded so reassuring and competent, I briefly considered increasing my daily rate.

"Thank you," Patty said, "and, ah, Mr. Rafferty, you really should do something about that cold. Your poor throat must be awfully sore."

"Good-bye, Patty."

After that I made coffee and sipped it while I studied Sherm Akister's photo. It was a wallet-sized snap, not very old. They hadn't known each other long enough to have old family snapshots. Patty had smiled at it fondly when she carefully took it out of a plastic sleeve in her billfold.

In the photo Sherm was standing at Kennedy Memorial Plaza. He had plump cheeks that sagged a little, but not enough to give him a hound-dog look. He wore a short-sleeved, plaid summer shirt, predominantly blue. There were two pens in his shirt pocket.

It was sunny in the photo, and windy, too. Sherm squinted at the camera, and his thinning hair was whipped to one side. He had a self-conscious grin, but there was a hint of pride there, too. Looking at the photo, I couldn't help thinking Sherm didn't particularly like to have his picture taken, but he was proud and pleased that Patty wanted to take it.

How's that for stretching available data to reach a conclusion?

On the other hand, I had at least some hard, cold, scientific data on Sherm, dictated by Patty and captured in my notebook. He was five-eleven, 217—the pudgy devil—he had brown hair, what there was of it, and brown eyes.

Sherm had turned forty-two last month, Patty told me. She had given him a set of shoe trees, a raincoat, and videotapes of all sixteen episodes of the old British comedy *Fawlty Towers*, because Sherm thought John Cleese was "just the funniest thing ever."

"You're a lucky guy, Sherm," I said to his photo. He squinted back with that funny grin on his face.

I didn't understand Sherm now, and that bothered me a little. I was glad he wasn't screwing around on Patty, but let's face it, being a whorehouse bagman and wetback smuggler wasn't a very big step up the morality ladder. Or was it?

I decided maybe it was partway up the ladder after all. Sherm might be cheating the system, but he wasn't cheating a person. That had to count for something.

I looked at Sherm's picture again, mentally factored in his height, and decided I'd recognize him when I needed to do so.

Then I phoned Cowboy.

"How-do, Rafferty," he said. "What's up?"

"I want to talk to a man tonight. He's going to be collecting the house cut from a small string of whorehouses. Chances are we'll have to snatch him."

"Okay," Cowboy said. "You got a place to stash him yet?"

"We don't need one. I want to talk to him for half an hour or so, then we'll turn him loose."

"It's your party. These here cathouses, they mob or freelance?"

"If there's any mob connection, it's very loose. These places may be mob-tolerated, but I don't think it goes any farther than that. Hell, you might know. The target is Manny Hinkston's bagman. A part-timer, not the regular guy."

"Heard the name, but I don't know anything about Hinkston, either," he said. "It don't matter. How much firepower on the opposite side?"

"Beats the hell out of me," I said. "There might not even be any opposition. Or there might be an escort for the bagman and door muscle at the houses. We won't know until tonight."

"Fine," Cowboy said. He pronounced it "fahn."

"We'll do it the easy way, whatever way that turns out to be."

"Mimi can't make it. She's down to Beeville, visiting her mama this week."

"No problem," I said. "You and I can handle it."

"I knowed that. I was saying, that's all. Seems a shame for Mimi to miss out."

"Life's a bitch sometimes."

"How 'bout wheels?" he said. "You want me to boost something?"

"Nope. We're okay there. The cops are looking the other way on this one."

"Hmmph," Cowboy said.

"The bagman's first pickup usually goes off about nine, so let's be in position by, say, seven-thirty."

Cowboy said, "Your place at seven, then?"

"Good."

Cowboy sighed. "Well, I'm gonna do this job with you," he said, "but I gotta tell you: If the cops don't care one way or t'other, it purely does take the fun out of it."

CHAPTER TEN

It rained for an hour or so late Thursday afternoon. By nightfall the clouds were gone, and a half moon had climbed partway up the eastern sky. The night air was clean and crisp and smelled of growing things. At least that's how the air smelled where Cowboy and I were, parked in the corner of an apartment-house lot, waiting to grab Sherm Akister.

"I swear, Rafferty, you are flat getting soft," Cowboy grumbled. "Next thang you'll be joining the police auxiliary." Cowboy is tall, thin, and so obviously country that strangers sometimes think he's role-playing. Other times they think he's James Coburn, but younger.

"I don't see the problem," I said. "I have to talk to Sherm anyway, try to convince him to go home. I need an angle for that, and I'm betting Sherm is ashamed of the dirty work he does for Manny Hinkston. That must be why he made up this spy crap. So if I lean on him and he agrees to snitch for Mancuso, then everything works out for everybody. Sherm can go home to Patty and ease into the real world, because then he would be a 'secret agent.' Sort of, anyway. Patty will be happy and still proud of Sherm. Mancuso will get to bust a piece of slime like Hinkston and—''

"And you get yourself a nice warm feeling inside." Cowboy grunted. "It's enough to make a man barf, Rafferty. And you best watch it. You're gonna get snakebit one of these days, actin' thataway." He wriggled around behind the wheel of his pickup and rolled his shoulders. Cowboy likes big handguns, and they're hard to conceal comfortably.

It had been a good idea to use Cowboy's truck instead of my Mustang. We were parked well back in the lot, nicely out of the way, but the truck cab was high enough to see over the tops of cars. We had a clear view of the entrance Sherm would use when he came for the money.

The apartment complex was more up-market than I'd expected. They were townhouse-style, two-story units, each with a tiny backyard inside a five-foot-high brick wall. There was a big yellow sun umbrella opened in one of the backyards. Cynical old me thought that might be an "Open for Business" signal.

I had gotten that idea when I checked out the area thirty minutes earlier, going in the way the customers, and Sherm, would. Up a walkway between two fenced backyards—the yard on the left had the umbrella—then through an opened wrought-iron gate, eight steps along a dim brick canyon between apartments, then hang a left, and there was good old number twelve. *Hiya, boys, come on in. It's a business to do pleasure with you.*

Large redwood tubs flanked number twelve's door, and there were thick bushy plants in the tubs. *Tall* thick bushy plants. But, of course, those plants weren't there to screen customers as they came and went. Of course not.

"Hey, that was a nice touch with the epoxy goop," I said to Cowboy. "I didn't think to bring anything like that."

"Aw, I keep it in the truck. Comes in handy now and again."

There were walkways into the complex every hundred feet or so. Cowboy had closed all the gates except the one we wanted Sherm to use, then squirted five-minute epoxy into the locks.

"Car," Cowboy said, as headlights flashed at the entrance to the parking lot. For the fourth time I slipped out of the pickup and started to walk toward the working entrance.

It wasn't a car, after all. It was a Jeep with a canvas top. An old Jeep, a restored military model, not the modern kind. The Jeep parked hastily and two young men of college age jumped out. I stopped walking and pretended to unlock the door of a parked Plymouth.

The boys looked around; then they walked rapidly up the walkway toward hooker heaven. One of them elbowed the other, and they both laughed. Their chortles hung in the clean night air after they'd disappeared into the gloom. I went back to Cowboy's pickup.

"Damn," Cowboy said. "Remember being young and full of piss and vinegar like that? Get a hard-on 'bout every twenty minutes, all the blood'd drain down out of your head; didn't have a lick of common sense. Damn."

"Oh, sure I remember. There was yesterday and last Tuesday and over the weekend—"

"Forget it," Cowboy said.

There was another false alarm a few minutes later. That was a Honda Accord driven by a florid man with a massive beer belly. He parked, got out, hitched up his belt, and swaggered up the walkway with the stolid air of a man about to perform an important task.

Not everyone had sex on their mind. Apartment residents arrived and departed, too. They were easy to spot. They carried packages or they looked bored or they were couples. One middle-aged woman rattled a Cowboy-sabotaged gate for several minutes, trying to make it open. Finally she went away, complaining loudly about rotten kids.

A slender, bookish man ghosted in, driving a spotless white Olds. He headed up the walkway, bustling along, eyes on the ground, legs moving rapidly. "Which is he?" I said. "Coming home from a hard day at the library or going to get laid?"

"Gettin' laid," Cowboy said. "But he don't like himself for doing it."

The college kids came out a half hour after they'd arrived. Their laughter was louder and freer now. The shorter one punched the other on the shoulder then danced away, boxer-style.

"You son of a . . . ." the victim yelled, giggling, and they began to spar in the parking lot.

Wouldn't you know it, that's when Sherm Akister arrived.

"There's your Chevy," Cowboy said.

"Stay loose," I said, and started for the entrance.

Akister pulled into an empty spot in the row closest to the complex, next to the college kids' Jeep. He was alone in the car. Sherm got out and stood by his car, looking at the boys. He wore a gray suit with a white shirt and a striped tie.

"Hey, Dave, wait a minute!" one boy said. "Ouch! Damn it, that guy . . ."

The boys stopped sparring, sheepish, then moved hurriedly to the Jeep, trying to run without seeming to do so. They did a pretty fair job at it.

Sherm had moved to the curb then stopped again. He watched the boys scramble into the Jeep.

Not me. I didn't watch anybody. I looked straight ahead and marched up the walkway, jiggling my keys. *Lemme see now, where's that goldarned door key? Doggone, I didn't realize it was this late. Hope Alma hasn't thrown out my supper.*

Behind me the Jeep's starter whirred.

Between the blank brick walls, in the gloom, I stopped and looked back. The Jeep had not started. The clunk and whir of the starter motor came and went as the driver repeatedly twisted the key. No luck. Sherm moved along very slowly, shaking his head a little, watching the boys try to start the Jeep. Which still wouldn't start. Arrgh!

Both boys got out of the Jeep and opened the hood. Sherm turned away from them with a sympathetic smile on his face.

Behind him, at the back of the parking lot, Cowboy eased between two cars, moving this way.

Damn! I didn't like having the college boys as witnesses. Maybe they'd be too embarrassed about their whorehouse visit to make trouble, but . . .

I moved farther into the complex, to stay ahead of Sherm. Cowboy was passing the stalled Jeep now, closing up behind Sherm nicely. All according to plan, except for the college—

"Bye, sugar. See you next week, hey?" The woman's words were soft but close; so was the low rumble of a man's answer. I realized the voices had come from the doorstep of apartment number twelve. The woman said good-bye again, in a loud whisper; then the door clicked shut.

The florid man with the beer belly stepped out of the bushes screening the door. He came toward me with his purposeful swagger. He jerked his chin curtly and winked in that male recognition signal that can mean anything from *howdy, stranger* to *damn right* to *see, I told you so*, depending on the circumstances.

"Evening," I said, and fumbled with my keys.

"Excuse me," Sherm Akister said, and tried to step between me and the guy with the beer belly. Behind Sherm, silhouetted against the parking-lot lights, Cowboy was covering his end of the Sherm-trap. His big western hat looked huge in shadow. Out in the parking lot, the Jeep starter whirred again.

"Sorry," Sherm said, and so did I, and we shuffled around clumsily. The space had suddenly become crowded, mostly because the guy with the beer belly stomped straight on ahead like he owned the place.

When all the "after you-ing" was finished, Beer Belly had moved on toward the trap where Sherm should have been, Sherm was knocking gently on the door of number twelve, and I was standing there with my face hanging out, feeling like a fool.

"How-do." Cowboy's voice floated up the walkway. He must have gotten one of those chin-shake greetings from Beer Belly.

"Ahhh . . ." That was Sherm, I realized, and I turned to

see him standing at the now-open door to the whorehouse apartment, waving me ahead. "Please," he said, 'if you'd like to . . .'"

He smiled encouragingly. It wasn't the leering, smarmy encouragement you'd expect, it was more like: *Don't worry, no one's going to laugh at you.*

"Uh, no," I said, "that's all right. Maybe in a little while."

"Sure," he said. "That's fine." He went inside and closed the door.

Sherm in the flesh was very much like his photo; an amiable schlump. Funny guy, Sherm. Probably the only "secret agent" I knew with a halfway decent reason for the con. It was going to be tough to lean on him later. Not impossible, just a little tough.

In the parking lot the Jeep motor finally started. The hood clanged when it dropped, then the motor roared and finally faded in the distance.

Cowboy ambled closer and leaned against the brick wall. He stayed inside the shadow. Cowboy had good moves. He said, "Don't reckon this one's gonna win any prizes for the year's best ambush, do you?"

"No problem. We'll get him when he comes out."

"I 'spect yore right, boss. We surely are due for it. 'Bout the only thang left to go wrong is the Three Stooges come out and poke their fingers in our eyes."

CHAPTER ELEVEN

Cowboy and I waited for Sherm Akister to come out. He'd been in there about twenty minutes when the door opened and the slender bookish man stepped out. The man hurried past us without looking up from the ground in front of his feet. If anything he looked more uptight and embarrassed than when he had gone in.

Cowboy shook his head. "There's a dude needs to find a better way to relax. Didn't do him no good at all."

We kept waiting. Three times people came up the walkway. Each time they walked past us, headed further into the apartment complex. One couple bitched bitterly to each other about the vandalized locks. Ronald—whoever Ronald was—was going to "get a piece of my mind, you can bank on it."

There were no new customers for the girls, though. "Mid-evening slump," I said. "Maybe they should get a happy hour going, build up a steady clientele."

Cowboy snorted.

Ten minutes later he said, "Curtain in the apartment across the way growing eyeballs, boss-man. I reckon we'd best make a move, else we gonna have folks out here getting in the way again."

"Might as well go in. Hell, it might even be simpler. I can lean on him in there, then we'll fade out. A nice, clean operation, strategically."

44

"Assuming he don't have any hard men in there who want to argue 'bout that, strategically." Cowboy grinned wolfishly in the shadows.

"Good point. What do you want? Front or the back?"

"You're the fancy-talker. Do your stuff; I'll cover the back."

He slipped away down the walkway; I went up to the door and pushed the bell. While I waited, a couple in their fifties strolled past. The woman smiled a greeting. I felt suddenly embarrassed, but what can you say?

You don't understand, lady. I'm not going in here because it's a whorehouse. I'm only going in to blackmail the bagman. Trust me.

I knocked then, because it felt more positive.

The door opened immediately but only as far as a security chain would let it. A short redhead with round cheeks put her face into the opening and smiled. Or at least, she tried to. It was a lopsided, tentative smile.

I smiled back at her and tried to look like a man consumed by the fires of passion. Make that a *generous* man consumed by etc., etc.

She said, "Oh, hey, I'm awful sorry, sugar, but we're closed, okay?"

Must have caught them with all the money out on the table, I decided. Time for Rafferty's Rule Thirty-three: Flexibility is the key to effective sneakiness.

"Naw," I said, trying for a mobster growl, "I'm with Sherm. Lemme in, for Christ's sake."

She looked startled, relieved, then terrified, all in rapid succession. Then she jerked her head back and slammed the door.

Almost immediately I heard her squeal. The door opened, all the way this time.

Cowboy stood there, tall in the small apartment living room. He held the woman by one wrist now, and she didn't like that. She clenched and unclenched her fists; her mouth worked nervously. She seemed ready to scream.

Cowboy's other hand held a huge Ruger Blackhawk vertically near his shoulder, the long chrome barrel pointed casually at the ceiling. He glanced at me but kept his attention focussed on an empty staircase that led upward from the other end of the room.

"You best git in here, Rafferty. We got us a problem with this here Sherm dude."

CHAPTER TWELVE

"Watch her," Cowboy said. "One of 'em already got away." He dropped the woman's wrist and went to the stairs, moving up fast and alert, the Ruger held ready. At the landing his booted feet stopped, then went on up in a rush.

The redheaded woman stood in the center of the living room with her fists clenched at waist level and her elbows held out from her sides. She breathed rapidly, gulping and shuddering, as she fought for control. She was twenty-six, maybe twenty-eight, and very pale.

"Take it easy," I said. "This has nothing to do with you."

She threw me a sceptical, hateful look and shook her head in a "leave me alone" gesture. Her hair was short but full and loose. Her hair moved out of phase with her head, a half beat behind, like a football helmet three sizes too big.

Upstairs doors opened and closed and boots clumped in sudden spurts as Cowboy checked out rooms.

I checked the lock on the front door and connected the security chain. The redheaded woman watched me, still gulping for air.

She wore jeans and a long-sleeved blue shirt. The jeans were fastened at the waist but not zipped. Only the bottom button of the shirt was done up. Her feet were bare.

It wasn't a particularly sexy outfit, despite her lack of underwear. She had probably dressed in a hurry. A skilled detective can deduce facts from the slimmest of clues. It's a gift.

Above me Cowboy's boots slowed and steadied to a walking pace; then he came down the stairs, cramming the big Ruger into a shoulder holster under his leather western jacket. Damned if I know where he found a shoulder holster that size.

"No sweat," he said. "Ain't nobody up there."

"Where's Sherm?" I said.

"This-a-way." He caught the redheaded woman's wrist again and brought her with us.

An arch in the back wall of the living room led into a kitchen/dining area. Kitchen right, dining area left, complete with table and chairs.

And Sherm Akister.

He was sprawled on the floor, on his back, beside an overturned chair. Someone had knocked him down, it looked like, then shoved a double-barreled derringer up under his chin and fired. The derringer lay on Sherm's chest. His suit coat was twisted under his back, mostly, and his shirt was open where two buttons had popped. His stomach was hairy.

Despite his rumpled clothes, Sherm looked almost peaceful. His face was a fraction more puffy than it had been in life, perhaps, but not a great deal. And the two little holes under his jawbone didn't look much worse than bad insect bites.

On the other hand, the back of his head wasn't doing the carpet much good.

"Aw, shit," I said. "Why Sherm?"

Cowboy pushed the redhead into a corner of the room. She slumped back against the walls, seeming to relish the support. Her breath was still noisy, but it wasn't quite as desperate. Her color was better, too.

Cowboy bent down to peer at the derringer on Sherm's chest. He was careful not to touch the stubby little weapon. "Twenty-two, looks like. Magnum, I 'spect. Which has enough firepower for that little job, all right."

"Shit," I said again. "What a helluva thing to happen."

"And looky here," Cowboy said. He toed a small cushion

between Sherm's ankles. The fabric matched the sofa in the living room. The cushion had an irregular smudge in the center of it.

"Gun was tight up against the skin, anyway," he said. "Cover it with the cushion afore you let it go off and the noise wouldn't be no louder'n a cork poppin'."

I looked from Sherm's body to the still-tense redhead to Cowboy. He shrugged. "Ain't nothing we did, bossman," he said. "Rest easy with yourself."

"Yeah, but . . . goddamn!" I said. "What was that about someone getting away?"

"They surely did." He stepped over Sherm to the curtained back wall of the dining room. He slid the tracked curtain aside but only a short way. "Sliding door here goes out to that little bitty back yard." He tugged the curtain closed again. "When I come around here to hop the fence, a woman was jumping down off the far side. She hightailed it across the parking lot. I didn't have time to go after her and still back up your play, so . . ." He shrugged again. "Sliding door was open. When I seen him, I figgered I'd do more good inside."

I turned to the redhead. Her breathing was much better now, though she still looked tense enough to twang if you touched her. "What happened?" I said.

She inhaled deeply and shuddered as she let the air out. I thought her respiration rate was going to take off again, but then she said, "Not in here with him. Out there. Please?"

"Okay," I said, and motioned her toward the living room.

"Don't grab me!" she said. She held her forearms up defensively. "Just don't grab me."

"No problem. Everything's . . . well, everything's not okay, but it may not be as bad as you think."

She nodded grimly and walked out of the dining room. She stayed close to the wall, and she was very careful not to look at Sherm's body.

She sat primly on the edge of the living-room sofa and bit her lip. Cowboy said, "Would you maybe like a drink, little lady?"

"Oh, god, yes," she said. "Great." Then, "It's in the kitchen, above the sink."

Cowboy left, and she chewed her lip again. Then she glanced down, saw her shirt and jeans gaping and sighed. "Don't get the wrong idea, okay?" She stood, zipped and buttoned wearily, then sat down again. This time she leaned back. "Should I be scared or what?" she said. "Because I am so fucking wrung out, I just don't know what's going on right now."

"I don't think you should be scared," I said. "Not of us, anyway. Did you shoot Sherm?"

She looked startled. "Christ, no!" Cowboy brought her drink—it looked like a triple—and went back out of the room. She gulped two long swallows of Scotch and said, "That's better."

"Who did shoot Sherm, then?" I said.

"I'm not sure." She had a puzzled look on her face. She took another big bite of the Scotch. "I can't imagine Becky . . . But that's her gun. I think." Another sip of Scotch. "I don't know what to think."

Cowboy came back with two opened bottles of Corona. He handed me one. "You like this Mex beer, don't you?"

"Beer is like sex," I said. "It's all good; much of it is wonderful."

"More Scotch?" he said to the redhead.

She shook her head. Her wavy red helmet wobbled again. "Not yet. Uh, what's with you guys, anyway? I mean, there's a *body* in there!"

"Well, now," Cowboy said, "you have to understand. We've seen bodies before."

She looked at Cowboy like he had an extra head then hit the Scotch again. I sipped my beer and said, "I need information, ah . . ."

She smiled for the first time. "Chantelle, sugar. Just call me Chantelle." She attacked the Scotch again, found the glass empty after that, and looked at Cowboy. "Please?"

"You bet," he said, and left the room.

"I'm certainly glad to meet you, Chantelle," I said. "I'm Lance Sterling. My friend's name is Rock Hard."

She blinked and looked a little sheepish. Four ounces of Scotch in five minutes had loosened her up a fair bit. Cowboy came back with the bottle and poured another triple.

She nodded thank you, then said, "Don't you like the name Chantelle, sugar?"

"Chantelle's a whore name. And I'm not your 'sugar.' "

She grimaced. "Okay. It's Lois. But who'd pay to fuck a Lois?"

"What happened tonight, Lois?"

"Shouldn't you tell me who you guys are and why you want to know?"

"No."

Lois swallowed a chunk of her fresh drink. "I guess I don't have much choice, huh?"

"No," I said again. That wasn't true, but why argue?

Lois shrugged. "Okay. Becky found him first or did it, I don't know which. I came down—"

"Whoa," I said. "Let's start at the beginning. Go back a half hour or so. Two kids came in. . . ."

"Yeah. There was nobody else here, so we each did one."

"The other girl's name is Becky?"

"That's right. Rebecca Chalmers. Look, she runs the place; I just work here. Well, I mean she runs it for that guy Manny what's-his-name." She was nibbling at the drink now; quick little sips at five- or ten-second intervals.

"Manny ever come around?" I said.

Lois shook her head. "I've never met him. Becky has, I think. I've only been down here six months, for god's sake. I'm from Chicago. What do I know about these Texas shit-kickers?" Then she looked at Cowboy, winced, and said, "Sorry," in a small voice.

"Okay," I said, "after the boys arrived, what happened?"

"Well, we were upstairs with them, one each, when Walter got here. See, normally there's three of us, and we work it out so someone is always down here to answer the door. But Glory phoned about seven. The curse, she said, though Becky said she was probably lying. She—"

"Forget Glory," I said. "Walter arrived. Walter is fifty, fifty-five, with a beer gut, right?"

"Right. It was my turn to answer the door, so I made the kid climb off, got a robe, came down here, let Walter in, and told him I'd be through in a minute. He said okay and sat down. Right here." She patted the sofa and smiled, fondly and a touch sloppily. "Walter's a sweet old guy. He's one of my regulars." Her second drink was more than half-gone now.

"The next guy was slender, mid-thirties. He looked like a librarian or an English teacher."

"I don't know about him. See, I finished the kid—the young ones are quick once they get started—and took Walter upstairs. I heard the bell, but it was Becky's turn to get the door."

"Maybe she let the slender man in and told him to wait while she finished with the other kid. Does that make sense?"

"Well, sure, because when Walter and I came back down, the kids were gone and Becky's door was closed. I figured she was banging whoever had rung the bell. That guy you're talking about."

"All right," I said. "Then Sherm Akister came."

"Boy, you guys were watching, huh?" Lois's eyes suddenly narrowed. "Oh, shit, you're not gonna bust me, are you? Because—"

"We're not cops," I said. Cowboy chuckled and pulled at his bottle of Corona.

"You sure?" Lois said. "The last thing I need is to get—"

"Trust me," I said. "Would a man with these twinkling eyes lie to you?"

"Probably, but what the hell." She giggled. Maybe Cowboy shouldn't have given her quite so much Scotch. He must have agreed; he casually moved the bottle behind his chair.

"Sherm arrived and . . ." I prompted her.

"Yeah, well, that was right after Walter left. They passed each other on the doorstep practically."

Cowboy butted in with, "Sherm was a regular, too, was he?" It was a good point. We had only Mancuso's assessment that Sherm Akister was a bagman. Police files have been wrong before.

Lois blinked stupidly. "Wha . . . Sherm? Christ, no, not that way. He only picks up the house money. The other guy—Bert or Bart, something like that—that animal keeps threatening to tell Manny we're holding back cash unless he gets blown a couple times a week." She made a face and shrugged. "We take turns. Who needs the hassle?"

"But not Sherm?"

"You bet not Sherm. He's straight-arrow." Her face changed, and she said, "*Was* straight-arrow. God, it's sad, you know? Why did she do that?"

"Becky? You think she shot Sherm?"

"Well, no, not really. . . . But I'm sure that's Becky's gun. A kinky john beat her up something terrible one time, she said, and she wasn't going to let that happen again."

"Where did you see the gun before?"

"She kept it in her bedside table. When I started here, she said we weren't supposed to have anything like that around, but she did anyway, and if I wanted to, she wouldn't say anything."

Cowboy rose and faded away upstairs.

"Lois, let's get back to when Sherm arrived. Becky was in her room, probably with the thin man we mentioned—"

"Right." It came out more like "rye." Nice Freudian slip, considering all the booze in her.

"When you let Sherm in, what happened?"

"Well, we said hi and how are you and stuff, and he sat down. He had to wait till Becky finished, because, like I told you, she keeps track of the money. There was nobody here to do, so after a while I went up to my room to smoke a joint. Which sounds like a pretty goddamn good idea right now, come to think of it."

"Later, maybe," I said. "Why go upstairs? Why didn't you smoke it down here?"

"Oh, Sherm caught me doing that one time, and he gave me a hard time. Not mean, not that kind of hard time. Not sweet old Shermy. But he carried on about how smoking dope would screw up my head and like that." She smiled loosely. "Sherm's a nice guy, you understand, but he can be a pain in the ass sometimes." Her eyes widened, and she held her hand in front of her mouth. "I shouldn't talk like that, what with him . . ."

Cowboy drifted downstairs then and eased into a chair. He shook his head. "Ain't no gun up there."

Lois said, "Well, then, I was right. But why would Becky . . . ?"

"Don't jump around. You were upstairs smoking a joint. Sherm was down here. Becky was in her room with a customer. Then what?"

Her drink was very low now. She sipped at it, looked at the level, sipped again. "Well," she said, "I heard Becky's door open and people in the hall. You know, when the two of them went downstairs. And a little later I heard a noise like someone swatting a fly with rolled-up newspaper. Either that or the big desk diary where Becky writes down the appointments. More like that, like that big diary being slapped shut."

"And?"

"And nothing. I finished my joint. Then, oh, two minutes, five minutes, I don't know, a little while later, Becky banged on my door and said I should get dressed. Hurry up, she said."

"How did she look?" I said. "Excited? Frightened?"

Lois shook her head. "Didn't see her. I was lying down, drifting a little after the joint. Besides, it was pretty quick. She knocked, said get dressed, then ran downstairs." Lois shrugged.

"Did you?"

"Yeah. Not at first. At first, I just lay there, but then I thought: Oh shit, what if there's a fire or some kink downstairs giving Becky a hard time? So I grabbed these clothes and ran down here."

She knocked back the last of the Scotch and held out her glass for another refill. When Cowboy and I didn't move, she grimaced and put the glass on the floor by her feet. "Thanks a lot," she said sourly.

I'd long since finished my beer; I put the empty bottle

beside her glass. "When we're finished here, you can have another," I said. "Meantime, stay alert."

"I am not drunk!"

"Good. You came down the stairs. Where was Becky?"

She looked at me peevishly for a full ten seconds, then said, "What the fuck. Okay, I came down thinking fire or fight, something like that, but everything looked okay. At first. Then I heard Becky fighting with that sliding door in the back. The lock sticks sometimes. She was cursing at it and jerking on the door. She was really frantic."

"Where was Sherm?"

"There on the floor, kind of behind the table. I didn't see him at first, because I was watching Becky and saying what's the matter and stuff like that." Lois folded her arms tightly across her chest. "Then she got the lock to work, and she opened the door. She looked at me, just for a second, and told me to get away. Then she went out the door. Gone. Just like that."

"How did she mean 'get away'?" I said. "Get away as in don't touch her? Or get away as in vacate the scene?"

Cowboy shook his head, and muttered softly, "Vacate the scene? Oh, my."

Lois nodded emphatically. "Becky meant get the fuck out of here, that's what she meant. And I saw why then. Because of . . . him." She gestured toward the dining room and Sherm.

"Go on."

"Nothing left to go on about." Lois hugged herself tighter; her voice was becoming weary now. "I started upstairs for my stuff. The doorbell rang. I went back and forth, up and down those stairs a couple of times, trying to make up my mind what to do. I decided to answer the door. You know that. Then when you said you were with Sherm, I panicked. Slammed the door, but Wild Bill Hickok here . . . What's going to happen to me now?"

"Pretty much whatever you want to, I guess," I said.

"I want to get out of here, that's what I want."

"Sounds a reasonable goal to me. Soon. Not quite yet, but soon."

Cowboy gave Lois one more drink; a short one, this time. She sipped it on the sofa while we talked softly on the other side of the room.

"How you wanna play this?" Cowboy said. "It's your tit in the wringer, what with every cop in north Texas knowing you was coming here tonight." He clucked his tongue. "Got you some mighty fancy talking to do tomorrow, boss-man."

"That's tomorrow. Tonight, I don't see her as the one who took out Sherm. Do you?"

"Naw," he said. "Way she tells it sounds about right to me. The little stuff checks out all right. There's a Baggie of grass and papers on one bed upstairs. Room stinks of it, too. And she's right about the other one, Becky, being scared of her customers. The gun's down here now, but there's still a can of Mace in each beside table and a Stanley knife under the edge of the mattress. Woman wanted to be able to fight back, all right."

"But did she ice Sherm?"

"Maybe," Cowboy said. "Or maybe it was that wimpy dude we saw come and go."

"Why?"

"Beats me. You the one with the fancy license. You figger it out."

Lois wanted to make a phone call before we left the apartment. I stood beside her while she tapped out a number she looked up in a worn address book. She chewed her lip and frowned while the phone rang for a long time. Then someone answered.

"Hi, Burr," she said. "It's Lois. Chantelle. Uh, remember what you said, about if I ever wanted to make a change?" She nodded rapidly at whatever was said, then, "Right, baby. I sure do. Got that. Sure. No problem, baby. Hang on." She clamped her hand over the mouthpiece and said to me, "Can you drop me off? A, uh, a friend will meet us."

"Where?" I said.

"He says it doesn't matter."

"Gimme." She gave up the phone, a little reluctantly, but without argument. "Mockingbird east of Central," I said into the phone. "Across from the Dr. Pepper plant. In thirty minutes."

His voice was deep and confident. "Thirty minutes," he repeated, then hung up.

There wasn't much Lois wanted to take with her; a couple of lacy come-on costumes, her baggie of grass, and a copy of *Cosmo*. It all fit into an oversize purse slung over her shoulder.

Cowboy found a grocery bag to carry the empty beer bottles and Lois's glass. He wiped the Scotch bottle and replaced it in the kitchen cabinet. We went around the apartment, wiping doorknobs and other places we might have touched, just in case some Dallas PD forensic man got overly enthusiastic. We turned out lights as we worked our way toward the door.

Then we were ready to leave.

The back door was the quickest, darkest way to the parking lot, but it meant we had to step over and around Sherm's body on the way. Lois carefully didn't look at him.

I did. He really did look like the photo Patty had given me. Which reminded me that I had to tell her about this somehow. Tomorrow was shaping up to be a genuinely shitty day.

Then Cowboy checked outside, said, "Let's do it," and we left.

It was almost midnight when we parked across from the Dr. Pepper plant, a few doors down from Campisi's Egyptian Restaurant. True. I wouldn't make up a name like that.

I hoped Lois's "friend" wouldn't keep us waiting. My house was only two minutes away; I was ready for home, a drink, a call to Hilda, and long thoughts about tomorrow.

Lois sat between Cowboy and me. She had shaken off her fright. She was up now, bouncy and cheerful. As soon as we'd gotten clear of the apartment, she had begun to chatter. It hadn't been a long drive, but we already knew more than we wanted to about her favorite video, her opinions of Tom Cruise and Bruce Willis, and the news that she was only hooking temporarily, until she got together enough money to go to dental hygienist school.

We'd been sitting there five minutes when a silver Cadillac Seville purred up and double-parked three cars ahead of us. A tall black man in a pale linen suit got out of the back seat and stood by the Cad. He looked over the car's roof, up and down the street. His face was stonily neutral.

"Oh, there's Burr," Lois cried. "Let me out! C'mon, c'mon."

I got out. She scooted over and got out, too. "Burr," she called. "Over here. Hi."

Burr's head swiveled our way, but his expression didn't change. He nodded once, gracefully slipped back into the Seville, and pulled his door shut.

Lois looked at me. She clutched her big purse and shifted her weight from one foot to the other. "Hey, thanks," she said. "Thanks a lot, you guys."

Then she ran to the Cadillac, tugged open the streetside door, and jumped in. The big silver car pulled away and turned right at the lights.

Cowboy watched the Cadillac disappear and clucked his tongue. "Tell you what," he said. "It must be awful god-damn scary to think you ain't worth no more than whatever the last dude paid to get your legs open."

CHAPTER THIRTEEN

Ed answered his phone on the second ring. "Durkee," he said brusquely, like it was his office instead of his home phone.

"Had a problem last night, Ed."

"Aw, Jesus, Rafferty, now what?"

"Akister's dead. In one of Hinkston's hooker apartments." I gave him the address, balancing the phone on my shoulder while I poured coffee.

A silence, then he said, "You do it?"

"No. And I don't know who did. I'll be in later and tell you all about it."

"Bullshit! You'll be in *sooner*, like right goddamn now."

"Later. I have to tell Patty first, then I'll go to your office. I'm leaving home now. Give me an hour or two."

Ed said, "You've just reported a murder and admitted you were on the scene. Now you're telling me you'll drop by whenever you get a break in your busy day? Goddamn it, Rafferty!"

"Look at it this way. It would take at least that long to catch me."

Finally Ed said, "Oh, for . . . all right! But hurry it up, for Christ's sake."

"See you."

"Hey, Rafferty," Ed said. "Now you owe me. Remember that."

I hung up and looked at the clock. Six forty-five; almost time to leave. I drank more coffee. It was bitter. I dumped the coffee and poured a glass of juice. That wasn't any better. The hell with it. I left the house and drove to Hilda's.

She was waiting, sipping coffee in her kitchen. She wore a subdued outfit; a dark blue patterned suit and a barely lighter blouse. It wasn't funeral garb, but it wasn't all that far off.

I leaned against the counter beside her stool; she put her arm around my waist. "You sounded terrible on the phone," she said.

I shrugged. "I hate this. It's going to tear her up."

She looked at me narrowly. "You don't have to be the one to tell her, you know."

"Yes, I do. But thanks for coming with me."

Hilda continued to peer at me. "I've never seen you quite like this before. Why are you so . . . not upset, but so . . . concerned about Patty Akister?"

"She reminds me of someone," I said. I stood upright and

moved toward the door. "I'll tell you about it later. The cops are screaming for details; I'm tight for time."

"We won't take both cars, then. I'll ride with you and listen."

Halfway to the Akister house, I said, "Patty reminds me of Edie Schuster, a girl in high school."

Hilda said, "Is this a twenty-five-year-old tale of unrequited love? Patty reminds you of the unobtainable princess?"

"Nope. It's worse. Edie Schuster was a junior when I was a senior. I was on the football team, and Edie used to keep track of my stats. Really. She followed me in both senses of the word. She would track me down and rattle off how many yards I'd made, first downs, all that stuff. That happened every Monday morning, unless she'd already caught me over the weekend."

We were southbound on Central Expressway, before the rush hour, thank God. The forty-mile-an-hour minimum speed limit still made sense. In another thirty minutes no one would able to go that fast.

"Go on," Hilda said. "Are you all right?"

I realized I'd been mentally back in high school, embarrassed and angry and, strangely, a little frightened as Edie Schuster stalked me through those crowded, noisy halls.

"She was a pain," I said. "There was the thing about my stats, and she used to bring me cookies all the time, and she'd hint that I should take her out. Very broadly, she would hint."

"But you ignored her," Hilda said.

"Did I ever! There was this cheerleader with long blond hair and legs up to here—"

"And big boobs," Hilda said.

"I believe you're right about the boobs. Anyway, I followed the cheerleader around like a robot. Me and my permanent erection."

Hilda said softly, "What was the blonde's name?"

"You know, I can't remember. How about that?"

"Indeed. But you remember Edie."

"Yeah. Edie. I tried everything to get away from her. Like you said, I ignored her. I pretended not to see her or hear her. I even hid from her, for god's sake."

The Fitzhugh Avenue exit came up, and I took it, swinging back over Central, southeast toward the Akisters' neighborhood.

"Edie embarrassed you that much?"

"She did. She *needed* too much, that was the problem. Needed *me* too much. Well, she thought she did, anyway. I didn't know how to handle that, Hil. I was seventeen lousy years old."

"It's a difficult time."

"Damn right. Anyway, one day Edie nailed me in front of my friends on a bad, bad day. I'd just flunked a chemistry test, I think, or they'd caught me smoking again. Whatever it was, it affected my eligibility to play. I was very uptight about it. So when Edie started yammering on about how wonderful I'd been in the last game, I blew up."

I let the Mustang coast up to a line of traffic stopped for a red light. In the car ahead, a fox terrier put its feet up on the back seat and yapped silently at us.

"I yelled at her," I said. "I told her I'd never date her, and I didn't even want to be seen with her. I was a real asshole. I told Edie she looked like her face was on fire and someone put it out with a sharp stick."

The light changed; traffic began to move. Ahead the fox terrier dropped down out of sight.

"Edie had a round face, almost chubby. It looked like it melted when I said those things to her. Her lips quivered, and tears came down her cheeks. Huge tears. I would have bet there were no teardrops that large. I remember she didn't even try to wipe them away."

I turned into the Akisters' street and slowed the Mustang. Hilda sat quietly with her hands in her lap.

"Edie stood there for a while, holding her books in both hands, crying. Kids were going by all the time, yelling, hurrying. You remember how schools were. Then, after two or three minutes, Edie turned and walked away. Or trudged away. Whatever. She seemed shorter somehow."

I let the Mustang crawl along the curb now. "One of the guys laughed. I already felt miserable by then, so I threw a punch at him, but he thought I was kidding. It just turned into one of those boyish scuffles in the hall."

I stopped in front of Patty's house and switched off the engine. Hilda said, "I assume you apologized to Edie. How did she take it?"

"I didn't apologize," I said. "Never had a chance. That day, when I acted like a jerk, was a Wednesday. Edie stayed out of school Thursday and Friday. I phoned her house twice; her mother said she was sick. I told myself I'd go see her on Saturday afternoon.

"Saturday morning she took her dog for a walk. The dog got away from her. The leash broke or maybe she dropped it, I don't remember. Whichever it was, she chased the stupid goddamn hound, and it ran out into the road. So did Edie."

"Oh my god," Hilda whispered.

"It wasn't a very busy road," I said, "but trucks used it sometimes, to cut across from the highway to a shopping center close to Edie's house. Anyway, she ran after the dog, right in front of a bread truck." Hilda grabbed for my hand.

"Damndest thing," I said. "The truck missed her. The driver rolled it when he swerved, but he missed her. An old man who saw it said Edie stood there for quite a while; stood there in the middle of the road and watched that bread truck slide past her into a power pole. Broke the pole, knocked the wires down; it was a helluva mess."

Hilda caught her breath and dug her nails into my hand.

"Then, when it was all over, Edie panicked and ran the wrong way. She got tangled up in the hot power lines. Edie never had a chance."

The Mustang's motor tinked as it cooled. Hilda and I sat quietly for a few moments, then I said, "I have to go tell Patty about Sherm now."

"Together," Hilda said fiercely. "We'll do it together."

CHAPTER FOURTEEN

Patty answered the door in a blue bathrobe made of some fabric that looked like light corduroy. "Oh, Mr. Rafferty, how wond—"

Then she saw our faces and began to tremble. "Is he . . . ?"

"Yes," I said. "I'm sorry."

Her eyes rolled up and she sagged. I grabbed her as she went to her knees. Hilda helped me move her into the bedroom. Patty wasn't quite out; she moaned and vaguely wrestled with us as we bundled her into bed. Hilda got a damp washcloth from the bathroom and began to wipe Patty's face.

"I smelled food cooking at the door," Hilda said. "You'd better check."

Patty stopped moving her arms and lay still. Maybe she was all the way out now: I couldn't tell. Hilda crooned to her softly. I went to the kitchen.

A pan of bacon on the stove was almost done. An opened egg carton waited on the counter, along with two slices of bread and a toaster. A glass of orange juice was half-gone. The condemned woman almost ate a hearty meal.

I turned off the stove, wiped it clean, threw out the bacon and juice, put the other things away. *How's that for service, Patty? I can't keep husbands alive, but I'm a whiz in the kitchen.*

"Rafferty." Hilda's voice floated in from the bedroom. I went back.

Patty was trying to sit up in bed; Hilda held her shoulders and said, "Rafferty's here now. Lie down."

"How?" Patty said in a hollow voice. "An accident? Not a stupid accident, please."

"No, Patty," I said. "It happened on his mission."

Hilda threw me a strange look then nodded sharply.

"Was it quick?" Patty said. Her eyes looked like the old photos from Auschwitz. "Did he . . . suffer?"

"No. He didn't feel a thing," I said.

"Who?" Patty cawed. "Who?"

Hilda said, "The enemy, Mrs. Akister. Sherm died in the line of duty." She glared at me like a bear with cubs. "He was a hero. We are all very proud of him."

"I'm going to find them," I said, and realized I was absolutely serious about it. "I won't let them get away."

Patty's head wobbled; she looked around the room blankly. Hilda pushed her back against the pile of pillows. She said, "He will do it, Mrs. Akister. Rafferty is very good. Almost as good as Sherm."

Patty nodded weakly, her eyes rolled up again, and she was gone.

When she didn't wake up after five minutes, Hilda and I went out into the hall to talk. "You go on," she said. "I'll stay with her."

"In a while, maybe. If she doesn't wake up and need me here. The cops can wait."

Hilda put her arms around my waist and squeezed. "I love you, big guy," she said. Then she went back to sit with Patty.

I found a bottle of Valium in the medicine chest and took it in to Hilda. "She might want these later," I said, "but let's hide the bottle until we see how she acts."

Forty-five minutes later Patty was still out cold.

"Her breathing and pulse seem all right," Hilda said. "She's probably better off this way, at least for now."

"Well, I'm hurting babe. There's going to be a uniformed

squad at the door soon, if I don't show up downtown. I'll see if one of the neighbors can stay with her.''

"No, let me stay. I'd like to, really.''

"You won't have any wheels.''

"I'll get a cab later, when she's better. Or when I find a neighbor to stay with her. You go ahead.''

Patty lay collapsed in her bed. Hilda had placed the cool washcloth over her eyes. Even so, and despite the years, she still looked a little like Edie Schuster.

CHAPTER FIFTEEN

I knocked at the door marked "Lt. Durkee" and went in. Ed held a phone to his ear. It looked smaller than normal against his big head. In one of his visitor's chairs, Ralph Mancuso slumped with his hands in the pockets of his leather jacket. He might have been awake; it was hard to tell.

"Forget it,'' Ed growled into the phone. "He just walked in.''

"Morning, Ed,'' I said. "Ralph.''

Mancuso tipped a languid hand my way. "Hi,'' he said finally. "Too bad it didn't work out like we hoped.''

"Where's Ricco?'' I said.

"Sergeant Ricco has a court appearance today.'' Ed was very formal; very irritated.

"Ah,'' I said. That meant it was a bad day to rile Ed. He became nervous whenever Ricco had to testify in open court.

Ed looked at his watch. "Nine-ten,'' he said. "You took your own sweet time getting in here.''

"The news hit Patty pretty hard.'' I dropped into a chair and yawned. Out late, up early, too much heartache. What a racket for a grown man. I said to Ed, "There's no hot pursuit element here. My being a few minutes late hasn't jeopardized your case."

Ed grumped. "I'll decide that. Tell me about it."

It told him. Everything. The truth.

"You let her go?" Ed said. "You handed her over to a new pimp and watched them drive away? Jesus H. Christ on a crutch, Rafferty. . . ."

"She was clean, Ed. You'd have done the same thing."

"Hell I would!" Ed rumbled and muttered, while I wondered exactly why I had let Lois go. Ed was right. I should have held her, called the cops last night, all that other good citizen stuff. But . . .

Lois hadn't killed Sherm, I was sure of that. The hooker we wanted was gone; she'd legged it away into the night. Ed had enough manpower to find Rebecca—Becky—Chalmers; that was the kind of chore police departments do extremely well.

Ed grunted. "I suppose you had that gunslinger Cowboy with you." He said to Mancuso, "They run together most of the time."

"Let's just say I was accompanied by an associate."

Mancuso nodded slowly and waited. Maybe he expected Ed to browbeat a name out of me. Ed waited, too, but he probably expected a smartass comment. I disappointed them both. My smartass quotient was pretty low that morning.

Ed said, "We haven't heard from the scene yet. Keep talking, Rafferty."

I described Sherm's body to them.

"That doesn't sound like a hooker to me," Ed said. "Holding him down, using the pillow to muffle the shot. Hell, it *could* be, but usually when hookers get after their pimps, it's fast and loud and messy. This sounds pretty calculated."

"Sherm wasn't a pimp," I said.

"Yeah, I know what you and Ralph say, but look at it from a hooker's point of view. Sherm was working for her man."

"Maybe so."

Ed held out a big hand to make a point. "And the derringer

is supposed to belong to this Becky, right? Strong circumstantial evidence there.''

"I wonder if the DA would agree with that," I said. "Though I'd like to know whose prints are on the gun."

Ed said, "Same here, and if they belong to the *other* whore, the one you let loose, goddamn it, I'll . . .''

"Never happen," I said, feeling almost eighty percent as confident as I sounded.

Mancuso stirred himself slowly and said, "But would a woman be strong enough? Akister was a hefty guy, as I remember. I don't think a woman would be big enough, strong enough, to knock him down, then hold him while she shot him, not the way you say it happened."

Ed pulled a face. "Juggling the pillow and all, yeah, that's a good point. Okay, let's talk about the customers Rafferty saw.''

I said, "It could only be the slender librarian type. The others left before Sherm went inside. And when I say slender, I'm not kidding. This guy is, oh, five-ten, about a hundred-and-forty pounds. I don't think he could have held Sherm down, either. Plus, he walks like he's scared of his shadow.''

"You were a cop once," Mancuso said. "You know how strong they are when they flip out."

"Yeah," I said, "there is that."

"On the other hand," he said, frowning, "Sherm Akister was no jock. I mean, if he tripped, over a chair or something, and landed on his back, he might be winded enough not to fight back. No matter who had the gun."

I though about that dining area and where Sherm's body lay. "It could have happened that way," I said.

"Then, too," Mancuso went on, "why kill Sherm Akister in the first place? Everything we have says he was like a big puppy dog, everybody's friend."

Ed massaged his chin. "Let's start with it being one of the hookers. Would Sherm hit on the girls, want freebies, anything like that?''

I said, "Lois says no. Sherm was a sweet guy; the *other* bagman wanted special treatment, though."

"Okay," Ed said. "For now. How about robbery, then?"

"I don't like that very much, either," I said. "If I was going to rob a bagman, I'd do it on his last stop, not his first. I'd wait until he was carrying all the money."

Ed said, "What if the thin guy didn't know that?"

"Assuming it was a robbery, he knew enough to be in position before Sherm arrived. He wasn't following Sherm; he arrived first. And if he knew that much about the cash pickups, why not wait until the last stop?"

We sat around looking at our shoes for a moment, then Mancuso said, "You know what we're working around to, don't you?"

"A pro hit," I said. I didn't like that idea very much. The guy had walked past Cowboy and me twice; we'd pegged him for a repressed wimp. That hurt.

"Aw, I hope not," said Ed. "If those jerks go to war, there'll be hell to pay."

Ed's phone rang. He answered it then passed the receiver to Mancuso. While Ralph talked Ed and I spoke in low tones.

"So Ricco's on the stand today, eh?" I said.

"Don't remind me," Ed said, cooler now. "Gorfus is the defense attorney. You know how Ricco feels about Gorfus." He rubbed his face with one large paw. "I hate days like this."

I nodded toward Mancuso. "Why is Intelligence working a homicide?"

"They're not. My guys are out there. But Mancuso sent an observer along, too, and he doesn't have to do the paperwork. No wonder he's got time to talk."

Mancuso finished his call and slowly trudged both steps back to his chair. "That was my guy Bromley," he said. "Here's what we have so far. If you don't mind, Ed. . . ."

Durkee waved him on. Rather magnanimously, I thought, since Ed would have preferred to hear from his own people.

"A couple of interesting things, Ed. Your men found the date book. The appointments are first names only and most of them are probably fake, but it's something. There was four-hundred-and-twenty bucks cash tucked into the date book. The house cut, they think. I agree. And Akister's wallet is still in his hip pocket. Scratch robbery as a motive.''

Ed said, ''Prints from the derringer?''

''Preliminary check only, Ed, but it appears to have been wiped clean.''

''The skinny guy,'' I said. ''Somehow he lifted it from Becky's bedside table and took it downstairs to ice Sherm.''

''Shit,'' Ed said. ''It's gonna turn out to be a payback from somebody Hinkston pissed off.''

Mancuso blinked his soulful eyes. ''I think so. Another thing. Akister had that Browning BDA you told us about, Rafferty. It was in his suitcoat pocket. Under him, apparently. They didn't find it till they turned him over.''

Ed harrumphed. ''Sherm could have fought back, then.''

''Not really,'' Mancuso said. ''The Browning was empty. Akister had a loaded clip, but it was in a different pocket.''

''That figures,'' I said.

''Hang on a minute,'' Ed said. ''I got something back on that gun.'' He riffled through stacks of paper on his desk. After a few minutes, he said, ''I can't find it, but never mind. I remember the gist of it. That Browning was lifted in a gunshop burglary four months ago, along with a dozen other handguns.''

''Hmm,'' Mancuso said.

''Sherm didn't do the burglary,'' I said. ''Betcha.''

''Naw, I don't think so, either. But this might mean Hinkston planned to enlarge his territory that far back. He might have had the guns lifted to pass out to his people.''

''Could be,'' Mancuso said. ''I don't like the sound of that.''

Ed agreed with him.

''By the way,'' I said, ''where did Sherm go Wednesday night?''

Mancuso was either deep in thought or sound asleep; who knows? I had to repeat myself. ''You were going to have Sherm tailed when he left the furniture store,'' I said. ''I know he didn't go home. So where was he?''

''Oh, he made the round of Hinkston's operations. All three hooker apartments, the hot car garage, and he spent an hour with a guy we think is Hinkston's newest recruiter for the shylocking action.''

"Calming 'em down," Ed said. "Keeping everybody cool for the war. And then the war started a little too soon for Sherm.''

I didn't agree with that; Sherm Akister wasn't the kind of person you sent around to soothe the troops. But I let it go. "Where did he sleep?" I said.

"About eleven o'clock he checked into a Motel 6 on R. L. Thornton. All alone. Didn't go out again; no one went to the room. Our team logged him out of there about eight yesterday morning. He stopped for breakfast then went to work.'' Mancuso blinked. "I haven't figured out what that means yet.''

Ed's phone rang again. He answered it, listened, then made a sour face. The conversation was mostly one-way from the other end. Ed stuck to saying "yes" and "sir" and "it won't happen again.'' Then he assured someone that he was extremely sorry—four times—before he said, "Thank you for bringing it to my attention, Your Honor,'' and very gently put the receiver back onto its cradle.

"Ricco?" I said.

Ed nodded slowly and said, "Ricco. During cross-examination, he called Gorfus a ratfucker.''

CHAPTER SIXTEEN

I left Ed's office around eleven and drove back to Patty Akister's house.

"She's still asleep," Hilda said at the door. "Come meet her neighbor.''

The neighbor and Hilda had been drinking coffee in the kitchen. Mrs. Holmiston was sixtyish, lean and spare and finely wrinkled. She had bright blue eyes and a clipped speech pattern. She looked like an ad for rural New England.

"Bad time for Patty," Mrs. Holmiston said, "but it passes. Did for me. Will for her."

Hilda poured coffee into a cup and handed it to me. "Patty's doctor will be here soon."

"A house call? Come on!"

Hilda smiled. "Mrs. Holmiston arranged it. She was very persuasive."

The gray-haired woman nodded her head sharply. "They're only body mechanics, that's all. Can't let them get too uppity."

"How's Patty look?" I said.

"Go see," said Hilda. "It's about time to check her again."

Patty lay on her left side with her knees drawn up and the bedcovers pulled tightly around her neck. The bedroom was dim behind closed curtains; I didn't realize her eyes were open until I'd moved to stand beside the bed. Patty rolled her head to wipe her eyes on the pillow, then resumed her empty stare.

Times like that, I always think of that old bull in the china shop cliche. Invariably I'm the bull.

"I'm very sorry," I said, which seemed inadequate. I couldn't remember a time when it hadn't.

Patty didn't say anything; she didn't look up at me. After a moment, though, her right hand crept out from under the covers and reached for mine. When I took it, her eyes slowly closed. She seemed to be sleeping after that, but her grip remained firm. We stayed like that for almost forty-five minutes.

Then the doctor came; the women shooed me out. I walked around and flexed my arm until it stopped feeling like a sack of wet sand. When my hand worked again, I went to the kitchen and drank coffee with it.

Eventually, there were "good-bye, doctor" sounds at the front door. Then Hilda and Mrs. Holmiston came into the kitchen. They both looked relieved.

"She's really out now," Hilda said. "He gave her a shot. She'll sleep for the rest of the day."

"You two can run along if you want," Mrs. Holmiston said. "I'll stay with her."

"Thank you," Hilda said. She sipped at her old, cold, coffee cup, grimaced and poured it into the sink.

"Rafferty, Patty thought she was pregnant."

"Aw, for Christ's sake."

"She went to the doctor yesterday. Can you imagine how she must have felt this morning when we showed up and told her . . ."

"You said 'thought.' So she's not pregnant?"

Hilda shook her head. Behind her Mrs. Holmiston did, too. They hadn't looked at each other, but their head-shaking was as precisely coordinated as a marching band.

"There was a lab delay or something. Patty was supposed to phone for the results this morning," Hilda said. She shrugged. "No wonder he got here so fast."

I said, "She could go either way about this, couldn't she? Okay, she's not going to have a kid without a father, but now she's not going to have a kid at all. Nothing to keep Sherm's memory alive."

Both women looked at me sharply. There was something arcane and female in both their eyes. I felt even more out of place than I had earlier, which was going some.

Finally Hilda sighed. "I thought she seemed relieved just now. But after she's had a chance to think about it . . . who knows?"

Mrs. Holmiston clapped her hands together softly and said, "No need to dwell on it. Need a few things from my house, then you two can go. Five minutes." She looked at each of us in turn, nodded to herself, and stalked out of the kitchen.

Hilda said, "Isn't she something?" We stood in the kitchen, holding hands, until Mrs. Holmiston came back. I gave her one of my cards, with my home phone number and Hilda's number jotted on the back. She promised to call if we were needed.

It was two-thirty on a Friday afternoon by then, a lousy time to go to work even if we'd wanted to. But we couldn't totally ignore it, either. "Plight of the small business-woman," Hilda said.

"And all this time the socialists thought we were having fun."

We went to Hilda's store first. She riffled through the mail, signed four or five checks, and asked Ramon to close up later. Ramon wrinkled his nose at me and hoped Hilda had a truly wonderful afternoon off. I told Ramon not to buy any antiques with Made-in-Taiwan stickers. He sneered. I snarled. Ramon and I don't get along too well. Suspicious detente is as good as it gets.

After that Hilda and I went to my office, where the steady march of commerce was about the same, minus the checks and Ramon. Then we went to Hilda's house.

Lunchtime had come and gone. I was hungry; Hilda wasn't. I built a ham and cheese sandwich and carried it into the living room, sat down beside Hilda on the big leather couch. She was asleep. Two minutes after I'd finished the sandwich, so was I.

We woke up around six, yawning and creaky, watched part of the evening news, and called Patty's house. Mrs. Holmiston said Patty had awakened, eaten half a cup of soup, and gone back to sleep.

"What about tonight?" I said.

"Taken care of. I'm here." Mrs. Holmiston acted like that minor detail had been settled long ago.

"We'll be over tomorrow then."

"Do that. She asked about you."

"You will do what you said, won't you?" Patty said. "Because they mustn't get away with it. That wouldn't be fair."

It was Saturday morning. Patty was up, sort of, sitting up in bed wrapped in her blue bathrobe. Her hair was uncombed, her eyes were red-rimmed, and she looked like she'd lost ten pounds overnight. "It really wouldn't be fair," she said again.

"Don't worry," I said.

"The police won't know where to look," Patty said. "How could they? Then don't know about Sherm's mission." She clutched her robe tighter around her neck and chewed her lip. "I wonder why we haven't heard from the government. You'd think they would . . ."

"I'm sure there is a great deal of activity behind the scenes," Hilda said. She was better at this than I was. Mrs. Holmiston, bright and alert as a rookie cop, was better at this than I was. So was a reasonably well-trained Labrador, probably. Or a pickled egg.

"National security," I mumbled to Patty, and immediately felt stupid.

Soon, mercifully, Patty said she felt tired again and closed her eyes. We tiptoed out to let her nap. Actually Hilda and Mrs. Holmiston tiptoed out; I ran like a scalded dog.

On the way home Hilda patted my leg and said, "Poor big guy. This is hard for you, isn't it?"

"Comforting new widows with white lies is not one of the things I do well."

"And you feel responsible, even though that's illogical."

"I don't know about that. I misread Sherm from square one. If I hadn't, maybe he . . . Yeah, you're right. But I still feel stupid."

"You can't fix every problem everyone has, Rafferty."

"Don't want to. Mostly, right now, I want to hit somebody, but I don't know who to hit."

"Unrelieved aggression," Hilda said. "You men have the strangest hormones."

"I could stagger up and down alleys with ten-dollar bills sticking out of my pockets. Sooner or later somebody would try to mug me, don't you think?"

Hilda smiled. "This is quite a need for physical action you have there, big guy."

"Or how about this? I start a fight in a cowboy bar. That shouldn't be too hard."

"When we get home I'll take you to bed if you want," Hilda said. "You can wear yourself out and not get covered with cuts and scrapes and bruises."

"Why wouldn't I? What would you do differently this time?"

CHAPTER SEVENTEEN

Saturday evening about seven, Hilda and I checked on Patty again. She was up and dressed this time, sitting in her living-room armchair. The TV set was on with the sound turned all the way down. Patty held Sherm's Ludlum paperback on her lap; not reading it, just holding it.

Mrs. Holmiston said, "Patty's much better."

Patty tried to smile. She didn't do such a bad job of it, considering. "You have all been so kind. I'll be all right, really."

"She wants to stay alone tonight," Mrs. Holmiston said. "Good idea. I'm only next door if she needs me."

Hilda nodded.

Like a dummy, I said, "Well . . ."

"I buried two husbands," Mrs. Holmiston said. "It's not easy, but it can be done."

When we left Mrs. Holmiston came along. We let ourselves out. Patty stayed in the living room, sitting in front of her bright, silent television, holding Sherm's book.

I thought that was pretty callous, but Hilda and Mrs. Holmiston disagreed.

"Let her do her crying in peace," Mrs. H. said. "Then she can think about what comes next." She nodded twice, turned, and walked toward her house with a stride more suited to a twenty-mile forced march.

Hilda and I went to Joe Willy's for hamburgers, onion rings, and beer. The food was good. The ball game on the overhead TV was okay, too. Funny how I kept losing track of the score.

I woke up in the early hours of Sunday morning thinking about the Browning Sherm had carried. It didn't make sense. I couldn't see Hinkston arming a part-time schlump like Sherm, even if Hinkston was planning a war with his competition. That was too much like letting a green recruit on latrine duty play with the cruise missile launchers.

I laced my fingers behind my head and stared up at the ceiling I couldn't see. Still fully dark. Quiet. Beside me Hilda's breath bubbled peacefully. Wonder how Patty was sleeping. Wonder *if* Patty was sleeping. Damned shame the way she got hit with it. Twice, in a way. *By the way, Patty, your husband's dead. Oh, yeah, and you're not pregnant like you hoped. Have a nice day.* Goddamn.

Maybe it was Sherm's idea to carry the Browning; maybe he wanted the self-protection because he was carrying Hinkston's money around.

Big money; a lousy four hundred bucks. And how protected was he with the pistol in one pocket and the clip in another? But that only showed he was an amateur, not why he wanted protection.

Then, too, the Browning was hot. And that was strange, too. I could picture Sherm walking into a gunshop and buying the Browning. But would he buy a hot piece off the street? Or had the Browning come from Hinkston, after all?

The sky had begun to turn faintly gray outside when I drifted back to sleep.

I surfaced again at eight, alone in the bed with my questions from the dark hours. I could hear Hilda in the kitchen; I had no idea where the answers were.

Sunday afternoon, after coffee and newspapers and brunch and a phone call to Patty—she sounded pretty good, actually—Hilda and I looked at each other and said simultaneously, "Would you mind if I . . ."

Boom-boom. She took off for Gardner's Antiques to catch up on what she'd left undone Friday; I hit the bricks to do some heavy-duty crimefighting.

Well, sort of.

I went back to the hookers' apartment, where I upheld the finest traditions of my trade. I impersonated a police officer. It was a moderately successful two hours; I learned a few things.

Most people did not appreciate being questioned twice in forty-eight hours, that was one thing I learned. If there really was a Dallas cop named Dougherty, I didn't do him any favors that Sunday.

I also learned that last Thursday night more people saw Cowboy and me than I thought. Their descriptions were typically erratic, though. We were taller, heavier, and considerably more fierce than either of us had guessed. Oh, yeah, and two people swore up and down we were black. Work that one out.

And I learned that the hookers were not such a secret, after all; at least eight people knew what was going on. Oh, now everybody claimed to have known what was going on, but I think eight of them really did.

And I learned that the slender man's white Oldsmobile was a 1988 Cutlass Supreme SL. So said a fourteen-year-old car nut named Josh. He had seen the Olds drive out of the lot onto the street.

"That '88 Supreme is an okay car," Josh said. "Except it only has a 3.8 liter V6, though, which is weak, man. Not enough grunt, even with a four-speed. Disk brakes all around, though, which is—"

"What was the license number?" I said.

"Huh?" Josh crossed his thin arms and screwed his face up in concentration. "Ah . . . did it have an H in it?"

"Beats me. Was it a Texas plate? Oklahoma? What?"

"Texas. Definitely." He seemed pretty sure about that.

"Don't try to remember the number right now, Josh. Just picture the back of the car. Was it a regular license plate or a vanity plate?"

"Whatta you mean, vanity?"

"Personalized. The kind that says DAVE-1 or STUD or MY JAG. You've seen them."

"Oh, yeah, right," he said. "No, it wasn't one of those."

I said, "Tell me about the person driving it."

He couldn't. He could describe the Olds down to the tire pressures, but the driver was only a man. I couldn't blame him; I'd been closer to the guy, and I didn't have a description that was a whole lot better. I slipped Josh a couple of bucks.

"Hey, thanks, officer," he said. "Awright!"

Now I had the youngest snitch in town. Maybe I could rent him out; he'd be dynamite on getaway cars.

After the apartment complex, I went downtown. Ed Durkee and Ricco were both off duty. There was a patrolman with a bandaged arm on desk duty. He kept one finger in the economics textbook he'd been reading when I came in.

"Lemme use a phone," I said. "Is Ed home, do you know?"

"You want to bother the lieutenant at home on a Sunday, you do it somewhere else, pal. Don't get me in the shit with you."

"I'm shocked by your lack of cooperation," I said. "And you a member of a proud force, our steadfast bastion against the rising tide of criminality."

"I got a number here for a shrink who does weekend committal referrals," the patrolman said. "How about I call him?"

I left Ed a note about the Oldsmobile. Maybe we'd find out there was only one white '88 Cutlass Supreme SL registered in north Texas. Maybe. I should be so lucky.

Next I tried the Intelligence Unit. Ralph Mancuso wasn't in, either, but a sergeant named Bromley was. He phoned around, found Ralph, then handed me the receiver.

"What's up, Rafferty?" Mancuso didn't talk any faster on the phone than he did in person. Southwestern Bell must have loved having him on their customer list. Imagine the long distance bills.

"I need a favor, Ralph," I said. "Where will I find Manny Hinkston's shylocking and hot-car action?"

"That might not be too healthy," Mancuso eventually said.

"I didn't know you cared. Or do you mean healthy for your investigations?"

"Both, I guess. What're you hoping to do?" A phone conversation with Mancuso was disconcerting; I kept thinking we'd been cut off.

I said, "Tell you the truth, I don't know yet. Poke around some, probably. It can't hurt to get Hinkston stirred up. Why let him hunker down and hide in the bushes?"

"It's a point. Okay, put Bromley back on."

Five minutes later I knew where to borrow a couple hundred the hard way or sell a hot Corvette. I still didn't know what I was going to do with that information, but I had it all written down. You have to start somewhere.

CHAPTER EIGHTEEN

When I knocked on Patty Akister's door at one o'clock the next afternoon, she opened it immediately.

"Thank you so much," she said. "I'm sorry to trouble you with this."

"No trouble." Patty came out, locked the door, and we walked out to where my Mustang dripped oil on her driveway. Patty wore a loose dark dress with a high neck. She had makeup on today, and simple earrings; neither made her face look festive, but they showed she was coming back.

Patty had called me early that Monday morning, worried because the police had phoned. Which funeral home did she want to pick up Sherm's body?

I'd spent an hour juggling calls to and from Ricco, the morgue, Patty, and a funeral home she picked out of the Yellow Pages. The post-mortem was complete, Ricco told me. "Ed says you picked it at the scene," he said. "A pair of twenty-two mags in the throat. One of them took out his brain stem on the way through."

"No hidden hypodermic punctures? No insidious poisons? No exotic Sumatran toxins on a blowgun dart?"

"You drunk or something? Of course not."

"Sherlock had all the good cases, Ricco. And to think they say life imitates art."

"Art who?" Ricco said.

The duty mourner at the funeral home promised to have Sherm picked up "within the hour, sir, and when might we expect to meet the unfortunate widow? To complete the," cough, "necessary arrangements?"

And that's where Patty and I were, cough, going now.

"How are you doing?" I said.

Patty shrugged and tried a smile. On a scale of ten, that smile was a three, three and a half. "Not too bad," she said. "I feel, oh, empty inside, I guess you'd say. According to Wilma, that's normal."

"Wilma?"

"Mrs. Holmiston. She says what you have to do is feel the hurt and not deny that, but at the same time you keep putting one foot in front of the other." Patty shrugged again. "I'm trying."

"Mrs. H. is quite a gal," I said. "And so are you, Patty. You'll make it."

She nodded sharply. "Yes, I think so, too. But then I think that means I didn't love Sherm as much as I thought."

"No, it doesn't."

"I hope not." She wiped her nose a couple of times after that, but she didn't cry. I didn't know whether that was good or bad.

The funeral-home guy was almost as smarmy as he'd sounded on the phone. The son of a bitch tried to unload a four-thousand-dollar coffin and a perpetual care plot on Patty not five minutes after she told him she wanted a simple cremation.

I cleared my throat significantly. "Sir?" he murmured. Our eyes met, as they say, and we reached an unspoken agreement. He sold Patty a handsome bronze urn, and I didn't make him eat his left shoe. Most things are possible if both sides will compromise a little.

Patty paid him with her MasterCard and shook his hand at the door. "Thank you," she said in a clear voice, and walked out with her chin high.

"You should have so much class, friend," I told him, and followed Patty to the car.

When I got there, she was already in the passenger seat. She blew her nose and blinked rapidly.

I said, "I'm proud of you, Patty. That was tough."

She sniffed and wiped again. "I'm going to make it," she said. "But it hurts so much. So very much."

As we pulled into the driveway, Mrs. Holmiston was knocking on Patty's door. Patty invited both of us in for coffee. The addresses of Manny Hinkston's shonky operations were smoldering in my notebook; I started to beg off. But Mrs. Holmiston nailed me with a glance that said I should stay, it would be good for Patty, and I'd be in big trouble with every woman on earth if I didn't.

Hilda can do that glance, too. Maybe all women can. I don't know whether they hold secret classes to learn that or they get special injections at birth.

Patty's kitchen was shaped like an old-fashioned keyhole. The long narrow part was a strip of vinyl-tiled floor with counters at each side, and the larger, round part of the keyhole was filled with a round table and four chairs. Mrs. Holmiston and I sat at the table while Patty bustled around, making coffee, and fussing with cups and saucers. Mrs. H. nodded approvingly.

As Patty was about to pour, the doorbell chimed. She looked flustered, but only for a second; then she scurried away to answer it. Mrs. Holmiston nodded again; she liked the way Patty handled that, too.

A man's voice rumbled through from the front door, then the kitchen doorway filled up with a hulk about six-four. He had hard eyes and a blue beard-shadow. He had a friend, too, who came in behind him, a blond guy with a sandy mustache that drooped down the corners of his mouth, bandito-style. Blondie was four inches shorter than the first guy but only marginally lighter. Both men wore gray suits that didn't fit particularly well. They looked like they'd flunked Sharing With Others in play school.

Patty brought up the rear. She looked confused but brave. "Um, these gentlemen work with Sherm," Patty said. She looked at them, at me, and back again. "Ah . . ." she said, and smiled quickly, mechanically. Mrs. Holmiston crossed her arms and looked at the men with a look I got too often from my junior-high-school teachers.

"That's right," the hulk said. "At the furniture store."

I stood up and moved away from the kitchen table. "Barcalounger buddies," I said. "Showroom sidekicks."

"Huh?" Blondie said. "Whazzat mean, Dwight?"

"I'm in the market for a living-room set," I said. "One of those leather outfits, I think. Give me your card; maybe I'll drop in someday."

Mrs. Holmiston said, "Patty dear, why don't you come sit down over here by me?" Her voice was calm and firm.

Patty took a few steps away from the men and toward Mrs. H. She said, "But . . ." then stopped.

I'd have moved a little farther from the two women, but I would have had to crawl up on a counter to do it. That lacked sophistication, I thought.

The biggest guy, Dwight, looked at me and worked his jaw a couple of times. Then he said to Patty, "We're all real sorry about Sherm, Mrs. Akister. We want you to know that."

"Thank you," Patty said. She started to say something else, then stopped and looked around, and up, at us. She seemed extremely vulnerable; a short, chubby woman lost in a forest of large men.

"Sure was nice of you guys to drop by," I said.

Blondie looked at Dwight for a cue; Dwight looked at me and worked his jaw again. He had coal-black hair, combed straight back. The backs of his hands were covered with black hair, too; and by the look of his knuckles, he worked out on a heavy bag full of anvils.

I decided to take Dwight out first, if it came to that.

"There's a little problem down at the store, Mrs. Akister," Dwight said. "We're missing some papers. Sales reports, that's all, but they're kinda important to the boss, you know." He *hur-hur*red an artificial laugh that stopped with the finality of a door slamming shut. "We thought maybe Sherm brought the papers home by mistake."

"Oh, I don't think so. . . ." Patty said.

"Not here," I said. "You can tell Hinkston I've had a good look around. They're not here."

"Who are you, pal?" Dwight said.

"Rafferty. I'm a friend of the family."

Patty was turned slightly toward Dwight then. I pulled my jacket open to show them the hip-holstered .38. "I'm a pretty good friend," I said.

Mrs. Holmiston stood up, took two steps to Patty, and gently tugged her back toward Mrs. H.'s side of the table. Patty's eyes were confused; the older woman's were not.

Dwight nodded slowly. Blondie glanced at Dwight, then he nodded, too. "Thing of it is," Dwight said, "these papers, they wouldn't hardly be worth having for somebody else. They'd only upset people and cause trouble. You understand what I'm saying?"

"I understand," I said. "How about I check again and get back to you? You can tell Hinkston I'll call him later."

"Mr. Hinkston doesn't like telephones too much. It's a whatchamacallit; a phobia. Maybe you oughta stop by, see him in person. Man to man, like."

"Good idea. Say, six o'clock?"

Dwight nodded, ponderously offered his condolences to Patty again, and they started to leave. Before they did, though, Blondie turned back toward me and made a mock pistol with his right hand. He grinned and dropped his hammer-thumb twice. Bang-bang. Cute.

CHAPTER NINETEEN

I followed Hinkston's arm-twisters outside; Dwight and Blondie got into a dark blue Plymouth parked at the curb. They drove away without looking back.

When I went back into the kitchen, Patty sounded off like a freshman journalism class. "What was . . . why did . . . who . . . ?"

"In a minute, Patty," I said, and grabbed her phone.

Mrs. Holmiston shushed and soothed Patty. Her eyes were bright and darting; she smiled slightly to herself. She poured coffee into a cup for Patty then set another cup at my elbow. As I picked it up Cowboy answered his phone. "Yo."

"It's Rafferty. Wanna go beard Manny Hinkston in his den?"

"Sure. He know we're coming, or is it going to be a surprise?"

"We have an appointment, you might say, at six. Let's hit the door at four-thirty."

"Where?"

"His furniture place on Garland Road."

"Good, it'll still be open then. With customers around, he ain't gonna have anybody set up to sneak up on our blind side. Not that far ahead, anyway."

"It's a parley, Cowboy, not a raid."

"Makes no never-mind to me. I'll keep 'em off your back; you do what you want."

Cowboy knew a used-car lot six blocks down from Hinkston's place. We decided to meet there at four-twenty. I hung up, drank a third of my coffee, and pushed the cup aside.

"Now, Patty, I have some time, but not a lot. Do you understand what's going on?" I'd been too busy working out how to handle Manny Hinkston; I hadn't thought about what to tell Patty. Anything that would keep Sherm in the clear would do, probably.

Patty frowned. "Well," she said, "those men didn't look like furniture salesmen to me, and I don't know anything about these papers they were talking about. Anyway, Sherm never brought work home."

"You're right," I said. "They weren't furniture salesmen. They're probably—"

"But you mentioned Mr. Hinkston, Sherm's boss. And whoever you called, you talked to them about going to Sherm's store."

"Well, yeah, but—"

"Oh no! They did that to Sherm!"

"No," I said. "Definitely not."

Patty looked at me suspiciously. "Are you sure? Because if I thought . . ."

"Patty, trust me. Neither one of them killed Sherm." And that was even true, which was new and different for a conversation with Patty about Sherm.

Mrs. Holmiston said softly, "Don't know what you two are going on about, but I think . . ." She tapped the side of her nose with her finger in that old "keep it a secret" gesture from the Christmas poem.

I had never seen anyone do that for real before. Because I'm a card-carrying opportunist, I tapped my nose, too.

Patty looked at both of us tapping away, trying to look sage and significant. Finally she sighed and flopped her hands in resignation. "All right," she said.

I got the hell out of there then. Places to go, people to see, things to do. If I could stitch together the right kind of deal with Manny Hinkston, Sherm could rest in secret-agent peace.

And then I wouldn't have to stand around Patty's kitchen doing jolly-old-elf imitations.

CHAPTER TWENTY

Hinkston Bargain Furniture was a white, concrete-block building on the southeast side of Garland Road. The entrance was on the left-hand corner of the building; the rest of the front wall was a series of plate-glass windows splattered with garish, cartoon-style lettering. CHEAP! was a word used often; so were BARGAINS!! and SALE! SALE! SALE!

There were a dozen off-street parking slots out front. I wheeled the Mustang into one of them; we stopped in front of a sign that screamed E-Z TERMS!!!

Cowboy snorted. "Easy terms, my butt," he said. "Knew a fella once was still paying for a kitchen table a year after the legs fell off it."

"Advertising license," I said. "It's not officially a lie if no one expected you to tell the truth in the first place."

"Uh-huh," Cowboy said. He checked the cylinder of his Ruger and levered it into the shoulder holster under his left arm. He took two full speedloaders from the side pocket of his fringed western jacket, examined them, and dropped them back in the pocket. Cowboy had a shotgun, too, an old twelve-gauge double-barrel with the stock and barrels sawed off until it was no longer than the Ruger. He thumbed two OO buck shells into the stubby little cannon, snapped it shut, and somehow tucked it away under his jacket on the right side. "Ready when you are, boss-man," he said.

"Wait till I hitch the mules to the ammunition wagon," I said. "We wouldn't want to run short."

"Might be funny now," Cowboy said. "You won't be doing no laughing if things git serious in there."

"Good point." By comparison I was lightly armed: the .45 from the glove compartment shoved into the back of my belt and a little Spanish .25 in an ankle holster. The .25 didn't throw much of a slug, but you can't hide much gun in an ankle holster. Decisions, decisions.

"Let's go git amongst 'em," Cowboy said.

We climbed out of the Mustang and walked along the front of Hinkston's building toward the entrance. A middle-aged couple passed us going the other way. The woman walked with her head down; she barely noticed us. The man did, though, and he stared. When I looked back at them, he was hurrying the woman along, half-dragging her toward an old white Chevy parked near the Mustang.

Inside a sallow salesman with a mustache and glasses took one look at us and pointed silently toward the back wall. Cowboy chuckled.

"Oh, damn," I said. "And here I thought we was sneaking up on them."

The building seemed to be one big, high-ceilinged room. All the floor area was taken up by furniture. Hinkston didn't believe in groupings and showy settings; this was the "sofas over here, beds over there, take it or leave it" school of merchandising. A few customers, mostly women, wandered up and down narrow aisles in the sea of tables and beds, sofas and bookshelves.

A loft jutted out from halfway up the high back wall. There were rooms up there, offices probably, with windows that overlooked the furniture floor. A raw-timber open staircase led up the loft.

The blond arm-twister I'd seen at Patty's house stood at the top of the stairs and watched us cross the floor. As we got closer he started down, setting his feet heavily to make the structure quiver. We met at the foot of the stairs.

"You ain't due until six," he said.

"I worry about being late," I said. "Sometimes I overcompensate."

Blondie sniffed. "I gotta frisk you."

"Oh, look, it makes jokes," I said to Cowboy, "while breathing through its mouth. Amazing."

Blondie reddened. He reached for his hip pocket then froze when Cowboy thumped him on the chest with the loud end of the sawed-off shotgun.

I checked behind us. Forty feet away a young woman in jeans and a Bon Jovi T-shirt prodded the cushion of a vinyl armchair, shook her head, and moved on.

"Let's not scare the customers," I said, and reached behind Blondie. He had a braided leather blackjack in his hip pocket. I tugged it out and showed it to Cowboy. "Excedrin headache number seventy-one."

"Well, leastways he cain't shoot himself in the foot with it," Cowboy said. He grinned at Blondie evilly.

Dwight, the black-haired hulk, appeared at the top of the stairs. "Get up here," he snarled. He didn't seem too happy.

A short man in a brown suit stepped out on the landing, too. "F'Christ's sake, Dwight, what's the fucking . . ." He saw us, said something to Dwight that I missed, and walked back out of sight. He hadn't looked any happier than Dwight.

"C'mon, will ya?" Dwight said. "He's ready to see you guys."

I pushed Blondie along ahead of us going up the stairs. Blondie snarled at me; he didn't seem very pleased, either.

Hinkston Bargain Furniture was a pretty grim place to work.

Manny Hinkston was in his early fifties probably, but they'd been a hard fifty years. His skin tone was terrible, his face was gray and wrinkled. His eyes were red and baggy. He kept a cigarette jammed between yellowed fingers, and every few minutes he clapped his hand over his mouth to drag on the smoke. The first time he did that I thought he was going to be sick.

Manny's hair was very thin, but he had combed it over his gray scalp carefully, as if there were more than a few dozen strands there. His baggy suit looked as cheap and nasty as most of his furniture.

Oh, yeah, and Manny Hinkston was a bullshitter.

"Hey, what's the problem here, anyway? I don't see no problem, do you? Do you?" A long look around his office, then, "Naw, there ain't no problem."

Manny and I faced each other across his cluttered desk. Cowboy and Dwight faced each other, too, as they stood against the side walls of the office. Blondie hadn't made the cut. He was probably still trying to figure out what happened and when would they let him play with his blackjack again.

I said to Manny, "The problem is the pressure you're putting on Patty Akister."

"What are you talking? Goddamn it, I got no beef with Sherm's old lady."

"Then leave her alone."

"Aw . . ." Manny slapped himself in the face with his cigarette hand again. "Look, you can understand this. You're a smart guy. You ain't no cop; not a real one, anyhow, which is why I'm leveling with you, okay? Sherm stole from me. And after I done him a favor, too. Hey, the guy's a newlywed, right? So I figure he could use the extra bread, a little something on top of what he made downstairs peddling furniture.''

Manny shrugged and scattered another layer of ashes on his lap. "And what happened? Sherm skimmed the take. My take! Why would he do that? I don't know. But he did it and that's that. Anybody steals from Manny Hinkston gets his lights put out, right? That's a . . . What do you call that? Tougher than a rule, you know, a . . .''

"A principle," I said. "A creed. A canon."

"Naw, not guns. You ain't paying attention again. A . . . a regulation! That's it. That's one of my regulations. Nobody steals from Manny Hinkston.''

"Which take was he skimming?" I said. "The whorehouses, the shylock operation, or the wetback run?''

Manny's eyes narrowed. "You get around, Rafferty. How 'bout that, Dwight? Don't Rafferty get around?''

A little more sunshine drained out of Dwight's day. "He gets around," Dwight said. He folded his arms. So did Cowboy. I wondered if Dwight's hidden hand was wrapped around a sawed-off shotgun, too.

"I'm thinking," Manny said. "I'm thinking it's none of your motherfucking business where and what Sherm stole. But—'' arms wide and a big grin now. His teeth were mostly brown. "—I can't keep secrets from people I like. And I like you, Rafferty. No shit. You're my kinda guy.''

I crossed my legs and idly scratched my calf. It was a way to keep my hand near the ankle holster. If they were going to make a move, it would come now, while Manny was telling me what good buddies we were.

Manny went on. "Sherm couldn't do it alone, you know. That lousy ginch Becky was in it, too. Had to be. Now there's another one who cheated me. I give her a good job, make her a goddamn manager, and she . . . See, they was skimming the Thursday business. Becky would 'forget' to put some of the tricks in the trick book. Sherm would let her get away with it, 'cause they were splitting it. Must have been. Else she was giving Sherm some of that pro pussy for his share." Manny cackled wickedly. "Naw, even Sherm wasn't that fucking dumb.'' He laughed again, louder, and set off a coughing fit that went on and on.

Dwight scowled at him. He may have been embarrassed. He should have been; he and his boss didn't seem very threatening with Manny coughing out his lungs and turning purple.

Finally Manny caught his breath and slumped back in his chair, his eyes streaming. When he looked like he might survive for another ten minutes or so, I said, ''Interesting story, Manny. Are you sure about all that?''

Bang in the face with his cigarette hand, puff, puff, then, ''You bet your ass we're sure! Ain't we, Dwight?''

Dwight nodded. He was sure, too.

I said, ''Let's say you're right. Why did you hit him in your own whorehouse?''

Manny winced. ''Aw, what can I say? It was a contractor did that. Stupid. Terrible job. And the dumb fuck didn't even do for the ginch, neither. I'm telling you, the kinda help you gotta put up with these days . . .''

None of Manny's rambling made much sense to me. It sounded like we were talking about a different Sherm. And we'd drifted a long way from the important point.

I said, ''I just want to keep Sherm's wife out of it, Manny. There's no reason for you to hassle her.''

''Hassle? What is this 'hassle' shit? Dwight went to tell her how sorry we all was about Sherm. So what?''

''Manny, remember me?'' I said. ''I'm the same guy from two minutes ago, when you said you had Sherm whacked.''

''Yeah, well, sure, I know that. But that don't mean I liked it. Business, that's all. And, see, the thing was, Dwight thought maybe Sherm had stashed the cash at home. So he asked the wife, all polite-like. What did it hurt?''

''It hurt, Manny. I'm telling you that Patty Akister does not have your money. I want her left alone.''

''You want?'' Manny said. ''Who you think you're talking to, Rafferty? 'You want,' my ass.''

''We can growl at each other all night and never get anywhere. All I'm saying is this: If you send your no-neck mouth-breathers around again, I'll send them back in an ambulance.''

"You could get sent somewhere, too, hero. Don't forget that."

I nodded. "Could be," I said. "That doesn't change anything."

Cowboy said, "Iffen you should get so lucky, there's still me."

"You see, Manny," I said, "if we go to war over this, you can't win. No matter what happens, it'll cost you time and money and people. And, in the end, you won't get your money back, because Patty doesn't have it."

Manny slammed his smoking hand over his face and sucked the last life out of that butt. He ignored me while he tossed the butt into a smoldering ashtray, fished a fresh cigarette out of a crumpled pack, and lit it with a red disposable lighter.

Finally he said, "Yeah, well, I think you're right about the dough, myself. I think that bitch Becky got away with it."

To my left, Dwight exhaled nosily.

"Dwight don't agree," Manny said. "But he knows who's boss, dontcha, Dwight?"

"No problem, Manny." Dwight didn't sound to me like it was no problem.

Manny looked at Dwight for several seconds then slapped himself with his cigarette and blew smoke across the desk at me. "Okay, that's it, then. Don't sweat Sherm's old lady. If she don't have the money, then she don't have the money. Becky'll turn up. Or, what the fuck, I have to, I'll write it off."

"For the hell of it, Manny, you mind telling me how much you think Sherm got away with?"

"Seven, seven-fifty, I forget exactly."

"You had him hit for less than a thousand dollars?"

"Aw, it ain't the money, Rafferty. It's the . . . what is it . . . the *principle*, you understand me? One wise-ass steals and gets away with it, then everybody takes a shot. A man can't do business that way. Seven thousand or seven hundred; it don't matter. People gotta pay attention to my, uh, my . . ."

"Regulations," I said.

"Yeah, them," Manny said, and he hit himself with the cigarette again.

CHAPTER TWENTY-ONE

"We know who killed Sherm, anyway," I said. "And why. That's something."

Hilda looked up from her fettucine Alfredo. "Excuse me, but does that really matter to anyone?" She wore a maroon clingy dress with a big collar that emphasized her jawline. Dynamite.

"It'll matter to Ed Durkee when I tell him tomorrow. Mancuso, too. He's been lying awake nights expecting a gang war to start." Then I thought about the possibility of Sleepy Mancuso ever lying awake, and said, "Well, he worries about it, anyway."

It was Monday night, three hours after Cowboy and I had left Manny Hinkston's office. Hilda and I were dining at an underground restaurant in downtown Dallas.

Hilda persisted. "But knowing who killed Sherm doesn't do anything for Patty's problem. Or does it? Maybe I'm missing something."

"Which problem? Widowhood, no. But the deal I cut with Hinkston means they'll leave her alone now. In Patty's mind Sherm can stay a secret agent and super hero."

The restaurant was one floor straight down from the sidewalk. The only things at street level were a valet parking desk and an elevator door. There was a reason for that, I'd heard, something complicated about deed restrictions and booze. Whatever it was, when they built the place, they built it underground, courtyard and all. What's the French for mole?

Hilda finished her fettucine and reached for her wineglass. "I'm glad you were wrong about the girlfriend theory."

"Non-operative," I said. "I've decided to learn from the politicians. Ahem. My earlier statements on the matter are non-operative."

Hilda smiled. "I suppose I can understand why he told her that ridiculous secret-agent tale. It would have been hard to tell a woman like Patty what he was doing for that Hinkston creature."

"Yeah, Manny's a real charmer, all right." I drank some beer. "Sherm could have quit, though. There are other places he could have sold furniture without putting in overtime as a bagman and wetback smuggler."

Our entrees came. So did desserts for the table behind Hilda, where a tall brunette screeched her delight for the eighty-fourth time. The restaurant was full and noisy tonight. The food was okay.

"So you're finished with Patty's case," Hilda said. "Are we celebrating?"

"Oh, yeah. Big win. And now, the dual award for Lies and Losing Client's Husbands. Drumroll. Bated breath. And the winner is—Rafferty! Wild applause. Thank you, thank you. I owe it all to the wonderful crew, my mom, and my podiatrist, Conrad. Fade to black."

Hilda smiled gently. "Bothers you, does it, big guy?"

I cut a piece off my steak. "There are loose ends, babe."

"Name two."

"Well, there's my old favorite: why the gun? What was Sherm afraid of?"

"I don't suppose you asked his boss that?"

"It didn't come up in conversation," I said. "Besides, Manny is lying or wrong, I don't know which, about Sherm skimming."

"That's an expert opinion, is it? Based on your long and close personal relationship with Sherm?"

"Okay, okay, based on meeting his wife. And what Mancuso told me. And the way the hooker, Lois, talked about

Sherm.'' I drank beer. ''And, all right, looking at his picture. And reading his bank statements and snooping through his house. All that nosey stuff I do so well.''

Hilda sat across from me, listening carefully, nodding slowly. Behind her the loud woman screeched again.

''And, hell, just the way I feel about him. Gotta go with the hunches sometimes, Hil.'' I sawed off another chunk of steak and put it in my mouth. Then I caught myself chewing like I was mad at the food, so I made myself slow down. Classy place like this, I should be more mellow.

Hilda said, ''But you said you were finished. You're not going to chase after whoever Hinkston hired to kill Sherm, are you?''

''Naw. Ed Durkee knows about the car—which will now turn out to be stolen—and frankly, I don't care that much. If Ed gets him, fine. If not, so what? The hitter was only a device. When cops catch a drunk driver, they don't put the car in jail.''

''What about Hinkston?''

''What about him? Sherm's dead; Patty has all the trouble she can handle. Suppose I went after Hinkston because he had Sherm whacked. Remember, by Hinkston's game plan, that was only a normal business practice; he's not going to surrender, stricken with sudden remorse. So suppose I went after him. Patty could get caught in the crossfire.''

''Surely you could hide her somewhere . . .''

''Oh, well, yeah. But I didn't mean that literally; I meant she would find out what Sherm was mixed up in. I don't see how I could tangle with Hinkston without that happening. Even if I nailed him cleanly—no shootouts, no blood-and-guts on Patty's lawn, none of that—the Hinkston-Sherm connection would come out in court. That would destroy Patty's image of Sherm. I can't do that to her.''

Hilda chewed fish. ''Hmm,'' she said.

I shrugged. ''So there you go. I'm stuck. Stopped. Anything I do now would only make things worse.''

''Maybe that's the answer, then. Stop.''

I shrugged again. Hilda winked at me and finished her fish. When we left a valet parking guy brought Hilda's BMW to us, all the way from across the street where it had been parked at the curb.

I gave him a buck, and we drove away. "We should have brought the Mustang," I said. "They wouldn't charge money to park a classic car like the Mustang."

"Uh-huh," Hilda said. "Where are we going now?"

"Lemme see, we've been out to eat and drink, so you'll probably be making a move on me any minute now," I said. "Rather than keep you guessing, I'll tell you straight out. I've decided to give in. You may have your way with me."

"Pitter-patter, pitter-patter," Hilda said. "That's my racing heart."

"Up, up, and away," I said. "You'll find out what that is."

CHAPTER TWENTY-TWO

"What do you think we do around here all day?" Ed Durkee said. "Sleep?" He waved my note about the white Oldsmobile. "For Christ's sake, my people talked to the same kid, got the same poop. We even found the car. Not that it's any business of yours."

"It was stolen," I said. "And dumped. Wiped clean. Betcha ten bucks."

Ed frowned. "Yeah, well, dumped, anyway. He burned it, so it looks like—"

"Manny Hinkston hired it done," I said. "He claims he caught Sherm with his hand in the till."

Ed smiled and leaned back in his chair. "Do tell."

I did tell.

After the first run-through, Ed phoned Ralph Mancuso.

He arrived within twenty minutes, a new Mancuso land speed record. I told my story again.

"But you think Hinkston is wrong about Sherm," Ed said.

I shrugged. "Yeah, I do. Not that it matters much. Sherm's just as dead."

Mancuso said, "I don't see how we can do anything without the contract hitter. Rafferty's testimony isn't enough, unless . . ." He arched his eyebrows at Ed. Would the DA go for conspiracy?"

"Forget it," I said. "Rafferty's testimony *isn't*, period. I made a deal with Hinkston to keep my client out of it; he might think I'd reneged if he noticed me in a witness box, sending him to the slammer. Some guys are funny that way."

Mancuso sighed. Ed said, "You can't keep this from Akister's wife forever, Rafferty."

"Man's gotta have a goal," I said.

Mancuso said, "What if she found out accidentally, because of our investigation? Would you testify then?"

"Nope."

"Why not?"

"Pure cussedness."

Mancuso looked at Ed with a puzzled expression. "Is he . . . ?"

"All the goddamn time," Ed said.

"But he can't. . . ." Mancuso said. "There are . . . We could lock him up, Ed."

"Tell me which cell," I said, "and lend me a rubber hose. If you're late, I'll start without you."

"See?" Ed said. "He's a real pain in the ass."

The rest of Tuesday went in dribs and drabs. I stopped by to see Patty. Her eyes were red, but she was determined to be gracious. We drank coffee and tried to make conversation that didn't involve Sherm or funerals or being alone or being married or being sad or the future, the immediate past, furniture stores, men, women, children. . . .

It was almost as difficult as it sounds.

* * *

Back to my office.

Mail? Some, mostly junk. Why get a fax? With mail the turkeys deliver their crud on their own paper.

Messages? One. Call Peter Kee. Oh, hell, the old fart must have shot someone again.

"Four times," Peter said on the phone. "Right in the chest. Can you come over and reload his gun again? If Pop does it, the next one might get hurt."

"Twenty minutes, and lunch is on you."

"No problem."

Peter Kee's grandfather insisted on doing the banking for the Kee family's suburban jewelry store. Grandpa Kee was eighty, give or take, a stern, old-fashioned Korean gentleman who proudly marched across the shopping center to the bank every afternoon.

The old man took it seriously. He packed a gun. And what a gun. Somewhere, years ago, he'd acquired an ancient, stirrup-latch Webley revolver. The British army issued them as sidearms for years. There was no telling how many Zulus and Boers and Huns and Johnny Turks had been ventilated by that relic Grandpa Kee carried.

"It was a Hare Krishna," Peter said when I got there. "Again. All that rattling and chanting and begging; Pop thought they were after the bank bag." Peter clunked the Webley down on the desk in his small office. "So Pop shot him. Boom. Boom-boom-boom. Four times." Peter shook his head. "I don't know what we're going to do with him."

I opened the Webley's ungainly latch, opened the gun, and took out the fired shell casings. Peter got a box of fresh ammunition from his safe and a shoebox of tools from a broom closet. I went to work on the shells. "Bet it scared hell out of the Krishna," I said.

Peter giggled. "I heard it; they were only four or five doors down. When I got there the Krishna's eyes were this big." Peter showed me how big. "He was grabbing his chest and carrying on about being saved by a miracle."

I pried the lead slug out of the new cartridge case and poured out most of the powder. There was a square of foam rubber in the tool shoebox and a pair of scissors. I cut off a scrap of foam and crammed it into the end of the nearly empty cartridge. "There's one miracle ready. Three more on the way."

The first time Grandpa Kee had pulled the Webley on an unsuspecting pedestrian, he hadn't fired, which was lucky for all concerned, because he had real ammo in those days. Peter took the Webley away and hid it. Three days later he caught the old man with a military Colt he'd bought second-hand. That was loaded for bear, too. Grandpa Kee sure did like firepower.

Peter took the Colt away, too, and he called me. We worked out a way to give the old man's victims a fighting chance. With almost no powder in the cartridge and no lead the Webley made a satisfying bang but that was all.

"Cops come this time?" I asked, working on another cartridge.

"Yeah," Peter said. "So we still have all that hassle to go through."

Today was the fourth time in three years the old man had tried to blow away a "bandit." This was his second Krishna. Besides them, he'd nailed a guy doing a street-corner detergent survey and an army recruiter. The recruiter wore fatigues; Grandpa Kee thought he was a terrorist.

That recruiter had been a good sport. He was the only one yet who'd seen the funny side of it.

I finished the last cartridge, reloaded the Webley with the phonies, and Peter locked the remaining good ammunition in his safe.

I said, "Slap leather, hombre," and tried to spin the lumpy Webley on my finger, B-movie–cowboy style. I almost dropped it. "Reckon ah need me a lesson from Fast Draw Kee, scourge of the West."

Peter Kee groaned.

By two-thirty I was back in my office, burping contentedly. When Peter Kee springs for lunch, he doesn't mess around. I put my feet on the desk and pondered heavy thoughts like the meaning of life, the imponderability of the cosmos, and how long a nap I should take.

There were no calls while I was out according to my service, and my case load was, ah, light. For light read non-existent. I was, as show folk say, between gigs. There was paperwork, of course. A bill or three here, a government form there. I could ignore all that. I was confident. I'd practiced.

A nice long nap, then.

I was deep in a spectacularly improbably dream about Hilda, me, a bottle of Wesson oil, and an empty football stadium when the phone woke me.

"Hargummm," I said blearily. Waking up was not all it could have been. And how could anyone's mouth taste like that?

"Mr. Rafferty?" a woman's voice said.

"If you're selling something, I hate you." My right foot was asleep, too.

"No. No, I'm not. Honest. Uh, I think—" There was another woman's voice in the background now. That voice was insistent. Then the tentative voice said, "Can we talk? I need help."

"Okay. Come on over."

"I can't," she said. "You'll have to come here."

"Well . . ." I once drove thirty miles to meet a nutty old farmer who wanted me to bug his chicken coop. He thought they were talking about him at night. Never again. "Give me an idea what the problem is, first."

"My name is Becky. Lois says you treated her pretty straight and I thought—"

The phone clattered briefly, then the other voice, the insistent one, came onto the phone.

"Hey, give her a break, will ya? She's scared shitless. So am I, tell you the truth." It was Lois, the hooker we'd found with Sherm's body.

"I get it now," I said. 'That's Becky, ah, Chalmers. The one who skipped out that night."

"Who did you think?" Lois said. "Listen, this is serious. There's all kind of shit going down now. Becky's really strung out here."

"How did you find me?"

"Burr asked around. You kind of stand out, you and the

skinny guy in the cowboy get-up. People on the street put us on to you.''

"Glad I'm not trying to hide out."

"Well, that's nice for you," Lois said, "but are you going to come talk to Becky or what?''

"I'll talk to her.''

"Thanks. You won't be sorry.''

"I'm beginning to doubt that already.''

CHAPTER TWENTY-THREE

The address Lois gave me was an apartment two blocks off Elm. Her new pimp's silver Cad was parked out front where the sidewalk turned toward the front entrance. A black man sat behind the wheel. At first I thought he was the pimp—Burt or Burr or whatever it was—but I was wrong. This man was heavier and harder, with a flat face and shoulders like football pads. He didn't look like the kind of guy you'd arm-wrestle for money. As I walked past the Cad, he nodded once, sharply, and pulled his right hand out from under a blanket piled oh-so-casually on the front passenger seat.

Well, well, well.

Inside the building, after I knocked on the door to apartment nine, they let me stand around while someone rustled and whispered and eyeballed me through the peephole gadget. Finally the door jerked open. Lois danced lightly from one foot to the other and back again. "Come on in, goddamn it," she hissed. "Hurry up!''

She slammed the door a quarter-inch behind my butt and quickly locked it. Then she fumbled a security chain into place. Then she checked the dead bolt again.

I said, "There's no sign of the big bad wolf out there. Besides, I hear he's into pigs."

"Very funny," Lois said, and headed for the back of the apartment. "Come on."

We went to the kitchen, where a tall black man in a light suit and a woman in aviator glasses sat at the dining table, drinking coffee. Well, the guy was drinking his coffee; the woman just cradled her cup like her fingers were cold.

Lois said, "Rafferty, this is Burr, uh, Roosevelt Burridge. You remember, from the other night? He picked me up? And Rebecca Chalmers. Becky."

Becky nodded shakily and said, "Hi."

Burridge stood up slowly and held out his hand. We shook. He sat down again. Somehow he made the process look like an athletic exercise.

"I remember," I said. "Dynamite suit."

"This isn't the same one," he said. His voice was low and mellow, as graceful as he was. "I only get a day at a time out of them. Linen bags so much with wear, right?"

"It's a helluva problem," I said.

Lois said, "You want coffee? Sit down, huh? And, hey, thanks for coming."

I said yes to coffee and sat down opposite Becky Chalmers. She seemed calm, except for the cup-clutching, but she avoided eye contact with me.

Becky Chalmers didn't look like any hooker I'd ever seen before. Her light brown hair was short, cut in a vaguely mannish fashion. Her face was broad and angular, with a firm jawline. Her skin was perfect; she wore very little makeup. All that, plus her aviator glasses, made her look like the manager of a wilderness store or an engineer or a NOW lobbyist. But not a whore. Becky—her name was wrong, too; she looked more like a Rebecca—definitely did not look like a whore. Which says something about stereotypes, I guess.

"My ladies think you're some kind of superman," Roosevelt Burridge said. "And that's fine by me, just so they get their pretty buns back to work."

"It must be tough," I said, "with all those dry cleaners to support."

Burridge let that one hang for a few seconds, then he waved a languid hand in that "let the games begin" gesture crazy Roman emperors made in old movies. After a two-beat pause, he snagged a magazine off a sideboard and began to leaf through it. *Gentlemen's Quarterly*. What else?

I said, "I'll let you know if we need any heavy management decisions."

His shoulders shook briefly. "You do that," he said, and turned the page.

When I looked at the two women, they were both watching Burridge. Lois glanced at me, said, "Well, anyway—"

"Lois thinks you can help me," Becky said. Her voice sounded like she looked: controlled, businesslike, low but not sultry. There was something else there, too, but it was well-hidden. Nervous energy, maybe, or fear.

"Help you do what?" I said.

Lois interrupted. "Stay alive! What the hell do you think she wants to do? For—"

"Hush, Lo-Lo," Burridge said softly. He didn't look up from his *GQ* when he said it. Lo-Lo hushed.

"Time out," I said. "I don't even know why I'm here. Let's start at the beginning. Becky, tell me what happened the night Sherm Akister got whacked."

She looked at Burridge first then at Lois. Finally she said, "Lois and I were working alone. Around eight-thirty, eight-forty, something like that, I took a john upstairs."

"Which one was that?" I said. "The college kid or the librarian?"

"The kid was before that. This was the, uh, librarian. That's a good description. He did look like a librarian at first. He came to the door just as I came downstairs from doing the kid."

I sipped coffee and waited. It wasn't very good coffee.

Becky said, "Well, the other kid was already down, waiting for his pal, so they left and I took the, uh, librarian john upstairs."

I said, "Did he tell you his name?"

Becky said, "Probably, but who remembers?"

"You went straight up? You didn't talk about anything first? Money; what's a nice girl like you doing in a place like this; anything at all?"

Becky started to loosen up. She relaxed her deathgrip on the coffee cup and put her hands flat on the table. Her fingers weren't fat, but they weren't thin, either. Her nails were clipped medium short. No polish.

"Well," she said, "the guy told me he wanted to get laid, that's all. You see, we try to get them into the room as soon as we can. That gets them committed, for one thing."

"It's private in the room," Lois said. "They don't worry about people seeing them; they loosen up and start thinking up expensive extras." She winked at me and grinned.

Burridge sighed happily over his *GQ*. Maybe he'd found a feature article on silk socks. Or maybe he was pleased by his new employees' experience with crotch capitalism.

"Okay," I said, "what happened when you got him into your room?"

Becky's face clouded. "Oh, God, I thought . . . I knew I was in trouble right away," she said. "He didn't want to talk or get undressed or anything. When I flashed him, he didn't even look. He just moved to get between me and the door."

She threw a quick glance at Burridge. "I, uh, had a problem like that once before, so I had a gun in the bedside table. I tried to get it, but he was too fast. He got the gun, instead."

"You'd be surprised how often that happens."

"That's what Burr said, too. But, probably, it didn't matter, because he had a gun of his own. Under his shirt. I saw it later. So, what I mean is, he could have shot me instead of just taking my gun away. It could have been worse."

"Tell me what he did next." I drank more coffee. It hadn't gotten any better.

Becky said, "He told me to sit on the bed and be quiet. Then he opened the door a little way and listened."

"He never said what he wanted?"

She shook her head. "I told him where the money was and said he could have all of it. He told me to shut up, and he kept listening at the door. At first I thought he was hiding from somebody. Then I thought maybe he was after the old man Lois was balling. That regular, ah . . .''

"Walter," Lois said.

"Right. Walter. But when Lois and Walter came out of her room, he just pulled the door closed, very quiet and sneaky, until they'd gone past." Becky looked down at her hands. "I'd forgotten Sherm was due any minute."

Lois said, "Hey, who would ever think of somebody shooting Sherm?"

Becky grimaced. "Yeah, but . . .''

I said, "Go on, Becky."

"So then Sherm arrived. With the door open the guy with my gun could hear Sherm talking to Lois downstairs. I mean, he had to hear Sherm; *I* could hear Sherm. After a few minutes somebody came upstairs. That was Lois going to her room, I found out later. After that the guy made me go downstairs with him. Sherm thought he was a customer on the way out, so he stood up and smiled at the guy. Before you knew it, the guy put his gun—*my* gun—in Sherm's face and started pushing him backwards across the room."

"Sherm had a piece, too," I said. "In his coat pocket. Did he try to get it out?"

Becky shook her head. "I didn't know that. No, Sherm was scared; his face went all white, and he put his hands up and said 'oh, no.' Or 'no, no'; something like that." She sniffed and rubbed her nose. "The guy, the librarian guy, grabbed a cushion off the couch and kept pushing Sherm back, toward the dining room. Sherm tripped, I guess, or maybe the guy tripped him. Whichever it was, he fell down. The guy jumped onto Sherm's stomach and he . . . The gun was quieter than I thought it would be, but I could tell when he shot Sherm."

Becky sniffed again, louder. Lois thumped a box of tissues onto the table. Becky took two, blew her nose, and kneaded the tissues into a tight little ball in her hands while she spoke. "I thought for sure he was going to kill me next, so I ran up to my room and locked the door. After a while, when nothing happened, I sneaked out—God was that scary!—and went downstairs. The guy was gone. I was pretty shaky for a minute, then I knew I had to get out of there. I knocked on Lois's door, went back to my room for clothes, and I ran. Oh, boy, did I run!''

I said, "I wonder why he didn't have you killed, too.''

She looked puzzled. "Well, why? Sherm, yeah, I can understand that. But how would he know what Sherm told me?''

"What do you mean, what Sherm told you? Manny Hinkston thinks you helped Sherm skim the Thursday take.''

"What! Oh, Christ, no, that's all wrong. Dwight was stealing from Manny; not Sherm! Big Dwight Stapner; the goon Manny keeps around all the time.''

"Dwight?'' I said. Somehow that sounded more logical than Sherm skimming, but . . .

"Yes,'' Becky said, her voice insistent as she leaned forward over the table. "And Sherm was going to tell Manny. That's why Dwight had him killed. But you see, now Dwight knows Sherm told me. I guess he didn't know then, but he does now.''

"What makes you think so?'' I said.

"Because this morning,'' Becky said, "Dwight and the librarian man tried to kill me.''

CHAPTER TWENTY-FOUR

Burridge leafed through his magazine while Becky began to tell me about the attack, but he listened. Lois listened, too, a mixture of fascination and fear on her face as it swiveled from Becky to Burridge to me.

"I was working,'' Becky said. "Burr set me up with a couple of tricks downtown last night. Afterward, about one-thirty this morning, I went up the street a little way to wait for Cletus.''

"Cletus would be the heavy in the Cad out front, right?"

"No," Burridge said without lifting his head. "That's Donald outside; Cletus drives my ladies on the hotel circuit.''

"Door-to-door service," I said. "With a smile."

"Not quite door-to-door. Hotel doormen are a problem. Some of them get nosey when they see the same car dropping women off night after night.''

"Anyway," Becky said, "Cletus picked me up, but a block later a car banged into us. It tried to crowd us into the curb. Dwight Stapner was driving; I saw him. And the man who killed Sherm, the librarian guy, he was with Dwight.''

"So what happened?" I said.

Becky said, "It really was kind of funny. I'm not sure how he did it, but we were up on the sidewalk for a minute, then Dwight's car went into a store window.''

Lois said, "Wow."

Now Burridge looked up. He smiled confidently. "Cletus drove dirt track for eight years. Speedway cars, demolition derbies, all of that. Nobody—*nobody*—pushes Cletus around in a car.''

I said, "So what's this about Sherm catching Dwight stealing money?''

"Well, he didn't really catch Dwight," Becky said. "The way it happened was Manny started complaining. I don't know exactly what he said, but Sherm got the idea Manny was having a dig at him. Implying that Sherm was stealing, you see? So—''

Lois couldn't take being quiet any longer. She butted in with, "Sherm wouldn't steal a week-old paper! That's so stupid.''

"I know that," Becky said, "but you don't appreciate how uptight Manny has gotten lately. If he thought Sherm or anybody else was stealing from him, he . . .''

I said, "And Dwight could whisper in Manny's ear two or three times a day, shifting the blame to Sherm. That would be tough to counteract.''

Becky nodded and straightened her big aviator glasses. "Right. But Sherm thought he could dig around and find something that would convince Manny it was really Dwight who—"

Lois cut in again. "Sherm loved that spy stuff. He read all those books, talked about them all the time."

I looked at the two hookers who were describing Sherm like a devoted brother. "Are you sure you two only saw him on Thursday nights when he came to pick up the money?"

"C'mon, Rafferty," Lois said. "Sherm was a nice guy. Sometimes we'd have time for coffee. He treated us like normal people. That doesn't happen much. In this racket, every bastard has his hand in your purse or up your . . ." She ducked her head suddenly. "Ah, sorry, Burr. I didn't mean you."

Burridge clucked his tongue. "Manners, Lo-Lo. Manners."

"Sorry."

Becky glanced at Burridge then hurried in with, "We got along pretty well, like Lois says, so when Manny acted suspicious, Sherm talked to me about it. I didn't want to see him get into trouble, especially for something he didn't do, so I said I'd help."

"How?"

"I started keeping a duplicate set of books. Well, not a full set. Just notes, because Sherm thought—Look, at that point, we didn't know it was Dwight. Sherm just knew he wasn't stealing anything. He was covering his ass, that's all."

I said, "When did all this start?"

"Oh, let me see, uhhhh, a month ago? No longer than that."

"And when did Sherm work out that Dwight was the light-fingered one?"

"Just last week," Becky said. "At first he tried to compare the figures I kept and what records he could get at in Manny's office. But that didn't help, he said. So finally Sherm decided to go around to Manny's other businesses and talk to people there."

"And?"

"And he did. He came to the apartment last Tuesday. That was unusual. I'd never seen Sherm except on the Thursday pickups. Oh, and at the store, of course. Anyway, Sherm said he'd been asking around in the evenings for a couple of days, and he thought he was on to something."

"He told his wife he was a secret agent," I said. "He told her that's where he was on Thursday nights. On the weekends he went north with wetbacks, too."

Burridge's eyes narrowed. "Hinkston's running wetbacks?"

Becky said to me, "You know about that, eh?"

"Rafferty knows all," I said.

"I think that's sweet," Lois said. "Sherm didn't want his wife to get the wrong idea, was that it?"

"Yeah," I said. "She's been, ah, kind of sheltered."

"Sweet," Lois said again, smiling.

Burridge frowned. He didn't think it was all that sweet. Or maybe he wondered how to get a wetback franchise of his own.

"So what did Sherm have on Dwight Stapner?" I said.

Becky said, "Well, he'd talked to people he thought he could trust, people who wouldn't tell Dwight. He said by the time he'd finished, he was sure Dwight was skimming a little here, a little there, off almost everything."

"What proof did he have? And what did he do with it?" Sherm's evidence would be the "sales reports" Dwight wanted so badly.

"He didn't have much," Becky said. "Right then. He told me he hadn't seen it all coming together until he'd finished talking to everyone. He was going back the next day—that was last Wednesday—to get the details. He said he knew then exactly what to look for." She shrugged. "I don't know if he went back or not."

"He went back," I said. "But I guess he talked to the wrong person. Someone must have contacted Dwight; Dwight talked Manny into okaying the hit; good-bye, Sherm."

Lois said, "Maybe Dwight didn't even tell Manny. Maybe Dwight set it up himself."

"No, Dwight told him," I said. "When I talked to Manny yesterday, he was disappointed the librarian hadn't hit Becky, too."

"You *what*?" Burridge said, and threw his magazine onto the floor.

Lois glanced toward the door; Becky went very pale and muttered, "Oh, shit."

"What's the story with you?" Burridge said. "Because if you're working for—"

"Relax. You'll wrinkle your pretty suit," I said. I told them about Patty and being hired to find Sherm; about meeting Hinkston and negotiating a truce. I finished up with, "My interest in this is very simple. I want to keep Dwight and Hinkston away from Patty."

Becky said, "I just want to stay alive."

"Lois might have that problem, too," I said. "You worked together; you're friends. Dwight would know that. He'll have Lois on the hit list soon, if she's not there already."

Lois winced and said, "Oh, wonderful."

After a few moments I said to Becky, "Why did you call me?"

"Lois said you were good to her that night," she said, shrugging, "and I thought . . . I don't know what I thought. I don't know what to do now."

"How many Donalds do you have?" I said to Burridge. "Hide the girls somewhere with a guard. In a month or so this will all blow over."

Burridge shook his head. "You don't understand. These are working girls. Becky, here, did a fine job on the hotel circuit the last couple of nights. And Lo-Lo's doing all right in a parlor of mine." He smiled at Lois sleepily. "If she ever learns to keep that mouth shut when it isn't making money, I'll get her some hotel work, too."

Burridge's eyes went flat and stony. "But nobody makes any money—not me, not them—if they go hide. See, this is not my problem. This is their problem. They brought it with them; they can fix it."

I said to Becky, "I know a police sergeant named Man-cuso who'd love to nail Hinkston and all his merry men. He'll treat you right; you'll swing an immunity deal easy."

Becky, Lois, and Burridge looked at me as if I'd spoken in Urdu.

"No cops," Becky said.

"Look, it's your best—"

"No cops!" they all said together.

"So what do you expect me to do?" I said.

Becky looked miserable. "I don't know," she said.

Lois frowned. "Well, can't you tell Hinkston that Dwight is the one stealing from him? We can't do it; Dwight wouldn't let us get close enough. But you could tell him. That way, Hinkston would get Dwight off Becky's back."

"It's not quite that simple. And the cops want to talk to Becky. That's why I think she should—"

"Why isn't it simple? Besides, that would help you," Lois said. "If Hinkston knew Sherm was clean, he wouldn't have any reason to bother Sherm's wife."

"But Hinkston wouldn't believe me. Not without proof of some sort. Anything else is a long shot, and I won't jeopard-ize Patty Akister with a long shot."

Lois sniffed. "Because she's a goody-two-shoes and we're just a couple of whores, right?"

"No. Because she's my client. She paid me money; I told her I'd help her. I owe her." I looked at the two women. They looked tired and scared. "I'll help you if I can. If there's a way out of this for you and Patty together, I'm all for it. But if I have to choose, Patty wins. Just so you know up front."

Lois flicked a sour look at me, then at Burridge. "Thanks a fucking lot, both of you."

"Shhh," Becky said. "I understand."

Burridge sighed. "Damn it! Look, Rafferty, I'll go this far. I've got a place in Richardson I can put them for a week. Can you do any good with Hinkston in that time? Because, the fact is, I wouldn't mind seeing Hinkston out of the busi-ness."

"No guarantees," I said. "I don't know that I can do anything. If I can, I don't know long it will take."

He grimaced. "Well, try," he said, and pointed at the women. "And only one week, you understand that, you two?"

Lois and Becky nodded. "Thanks, Burr."

Burridge snorted. "I must be getting soft. I swear, ladies, when this is over, you're going to work your buns off, just to catch up."

They both nodded again. "Okay," Becky said. "No problem."

I asked Becky more questions about Sherm's amateur sleuthing expedition. She had no idea what he'd found; she hadn't seen any notes; she didn't know where Sherm might have hidden the "proof"; she wasn't sure it even existed.

Finally, a little before seven, I stood up, ready to leave the apartment. Burridge said, "You go ahead. We'll be going, too, in a little while."

"When I came here I didn't know there was active opposition. I don't think I was tailed, but . . . If you want, I'll hang around, help cover the girls on the way out."

Burridge chuckled gently. "No need. Donald's out front. Got another man in back. Everything's under control."

"Hey, what does Donald have under that blanket in the Cad? Shotgun? Uzi?"

Burridge smiled. "A brand-new HK. Donald's a very cool dude. He says Uzis are passé."

CHAPTER TWENTY-FIVE

I found a phone six blocks from the apartment and phoned Hilda's house. No answer. I phoned my house.

"Hello," she said.

"How about that? A burglar who answers the phone. I'll be right over to interrogate you."

"I'll never talk," Hilda said, "even if you rip off all my clothes, and paw my tender body, and perform exotic sexual—"

"Take it easy, babe. I don't want to get stuck in this phone booth. I'll bring food; you pick what."

"I brought Chinese. Lemon chicken, sweet-and-sour pork, and Singapore noodles. It's in the oven, staying warm."

"Way to go. I'll be right there."

Hilda chuckled and suggested a few things we might do after dinner. "*Now* try to get out of that phone booth."

"Uh-oh. Ah, I could think about cold showers, I suppose."

"Or oatmeal."

"The IRS."

"Radical feminists," Hilda said.

"That one worked," I said. "I'll be right there."

Hilda pushed her empty plate away and reached for her wineglass. "But I thought you were going to leave it alone," she said. "Because there was no way to get whoever killed Sherm without Patty finding out about—well, you know what I mean."

"I know. Trouble is, now I know who did it. And that makes it harder to ignore. But the main reason is, I think Dwight will keep pushing until he nails one or both of the hookers."

"They have a pimp. Aren't pimps supposed to protect their girls?"

I shrugged and reached for more Singapore noodles. "Burridge is protecting them, for now. But he doesn't seem to feel much obligation. He says this situation did not arise while they were in his employ."

Hilda shook her head. "Did not arise? He doesn't talk like that, surely."

"Well, okay, not quite. But close. Guy looks more like a stockbroker than a pimp."

"Then he might want to protect his investment," she said.

"Maybe. But then again, he might talk himself into cutting his losses, instead."

"You mean he would hand those women over to this Dwight creature?"

"Not hand over. But if this thing doesn't clear up in a week or two, I can see Burridge turning the girls out onto the street, which amounts to the same thing."

Hilda sighed. "Can you help these women and still keep Sherm's background from Patty?"

"I sure as hell hope so."

Cat meowed at the back door; I let him in. He went straight to the refrigerator, sat in front of it, and meowed loudly.

"Trained him myself," I told Hilda. "If he wants milk, he has to ask for it." Cat meowed again, louder. I poured milk into a bowl for him. Funny, he seemed to be putting on weight these days.

"You trained *him*? Hah! The cat has trained you. You hear a meow, you give him milk. And, really, you shouldn't feed him so much."

"It's not me; it's that dippy broad behind me. She gives him canned stuff all the time."

"Well, whoever's doing it, the cat is too fat, Rafferty."

I looked down at him lapping the milk. "Muscle, that's all that is. Fifteen pounds of rippling muscle."

The late television news had a story about a stolen car that had crashed and been abandoned downtown. They ran film of a dark Honda Accord half-in and half-out of a store window. All they needed was a little animated scoreboard. Cletus 1; Dwight 0.

Another shot showed what appeared to be bodies strewn under and around the car. Then I realized they were only mannequins. The talking head doing the newscast carried on about "dummies" and "dropping in unexpectedly," but it didn't seem very funny to me.

I kept thinking that Dwight Stapner wouldn't feel happy— or safe—until they were bodies.

Sherm Akister's funeral was held the next morning in a small chapel attached to a crematory. Hilda and I sat with Patty during the ceremony. So did Sherm's sister. Meg was a large woman in her late forties with a grim expression. She had flown in that morning from Atlanta. Meg didn't say much.

Old Mrs. Holmiston sat beside me. She kept scowling at Sherm's sister and shaking her head.

Two men from Hinkston's furniture store came to the funeral. They said they were fellow salesmen. I think they really were.

Dwight Stapner was there. He sat in the back, well away from the rest of us. Manny Hinkston didn't show; neither did Becky or Lois.

And that was it. Eight mourners, plus a skinny, ring-in preacher who opened his mouth and immediately proved he didn't know Sherm Akister from a '67 Plymouth.

And Sherm, of course, in a closed casket.

Oh, and there was a funeral home smoothie who choreographed the affair. He ushered us in, stood up and sat down at the right times, and, afterward, he shooed us out like befuddled sheep.

Out front we stood around, blinking at the sunlight and feeling uncomfortable. Then the salesmen and the preacher offered their condolences to Patty and Sherm's sister. The salesmen seemed genuine enough, and even the preacher had the good grace to look embarrassed when Patty slipped him his honorarium. So that part of it went okay.

Dwight didn't approach Patty. I'm not saying my expression had anything to do with that, but Hilda poked me and hissed, "Stop that. Right now!"

And then it was over.

Patty wanted Sherm's sister to come to the house, but Meg said no. Had to catch a plane, she said. Had to get back to the family.

I offered her a ride to the airport, but she wouldn't accept that, either. Forty-five minutes after the ceremony had started, the cab she'd arranged pulled up. She and Patty hugged, without either one of them putting her heart into it, and sister Meg left, still grim. Strange woman.

The furniture salesmen were long gone by then, and the funeral home guy had started to harrumph at us. So we all got into Hilda's BMW and went to Patty's house.

Mrs. Holmiston and Hilda came up with a plate of nibble-stuff and coffee. We sat in the living room and looked at each other. No one said anything for a long time.

"I, uh, I still don't understand why I haven't heard from the government," Patty said. "You'd think—"

"Slow," Mrs. Holmiston said firmly. "Never saw a government do anything in a hurry. Don't you worry about it, dear." She gave me a sly little wink.

"Well . . ."

Hilda said, "Patty, I don't mean to pry, but are you all right for, um, money?"

"Oh, please," Patty said. "I'm fine. Don't worry about me. No, I have my savings, and Sherm had life insurance. A new policy, but the man said I should get the check soon."

Mrs. Holmiston snorted. "Belive it when you see it. Insurance companies can be as slow as government."

After that we just sat around and talked about the weather and what a great guy Sherm had been.

It was a little better than root-canal work, but not much.

CHAPTER TWENTY-SIX

Someone in Ed's office said he was working a holdup homicide at an address not far off Mockingbird Lane. I found it easily. It was a one-hour dry-cleaning place with a pale young patrolman guarding the door. He worked his mouth and swallowed a lot.

I showed him my PI license and said, "Ed Durkee here? Or Ricco?"

He started to look over his shoulder into the store then stopped himself. He swallowed again. "Lieutenant Durkee's inside. I think Sergeant Ricco is around somewhere, but I'm not supposed to let—"

"He's okay, kid," Ricco said behind me. "Come on in, Rafferty."

As we went past the young cop, Ricco whispered, "Strawberry milkshake. Rhubarb pie."

The cop gulped; Ricco cackled. "Ed's in the back," he said to me. "Watch where you step."

An old man's body lay crumpled behind the counter, half covered with plastic-sheathed clothes he must have dragged off the motorized racks when he went down. The right side of his face wasn't there anymore.

"Helluva mess, ain't it?" Ricco said. "Shotgun, looks like. Fucking punks."

He led the way down a narrow path in the forest of hanging

suits and dresses. Behind the clothes, against the back wall of the small building, there was a small rest area with a sink and a table and chairs. Ed Durkee, a policewoman, and a gray-haired woman sat at the table. The older woman sobbed into her hands; Ed looked even more like a weary hound dog than he usually did. The policewoman said, "There, there."

Ed looked up at Ricco and me, nodded shortly, and got up. "I'm sorry," he said to the crying woman.

She bobbed her head twice, but she didn't stop crying, and she didn't take her hands away from her face. Ed patted her shoulder twice, clumsily; then he motioned me away, ahead of him. The policewoman said, "There, there," again.

We stopped in the midst of the clothes forest. Ed dry-washed his rubbery face. "Goddamn it, anyway, Ricco, what have you got?"

Ricco pawed through a pocket notebook. "Two male caucs," he said. "One maybe nineteen, twenty; the other a little younger. Guy two doors down says they got into an old Cougar, headed west. He didn't get the plate number, what else? The Cougar was a heap, he says. Gray primer on the right-side door. Busted muffler. I called it in already."

Ed nodded and crammed his hands into the pockets of his brown suitcoat. "They got away with eighty bucks. How about that?" He shook his head irritably and growled at me, "What the hell do you want?"

"It can wait, Ed. You have your hands—"

"We can't do any more until Forensics gets here, anyway. Let's go outside."

A small crowd had gathered on the sidewalk. We pushed through the people, crossed the street, and leaned against my Mustang.

"I need a diversion, Rafferty. Divert me."

"I know who had Sherm Akister whacked," I said. "And he's not finished yet." I told Ed and Ricco about Dwight Stapner, Becky, Roosevelt Burridge, etc, etc.

"Nice to know, I guess," Ed said. "Where is she now?"

"Beats me. Hiding out."

"Will she come in? Her testimony would be only hearsay, but . . ."

"I told her to come in," I said. "She won't. Later, maybe, but not yet."

"Uh-huh."

I said, "I should ask Mancuso this, but I can't find him. Exactly how strong are Hinkston's mob connections? Because if he's not really one of them, then—"

Ricco cut in with a savage grin. "Then you could just take out Hinkston *and* this Dwight prick. Problem solved. Tell you what, I like it."

"Actually I was thinking more of siccing you guys onto them," I said. "I'd help, of course."

Ed snorted. "That's what you were thinking, was it? Bet that wasn't what your pal Cowboy was thinking."

"I wouldn't know."

That was a lie. I did know. Cowboy would agree with Ricco; he'd just phrase it differently. *Blow them suckers away,* he'd say. That or something equally down-home.

"See, Ed, I figured that with good solid charges against them, Hinkston and Dwight would be too exposed to go after Becky, and they'd be too busy to bother Patty."

Ed shrugged. "I don't think it would work out that way. Mancuso's report says Hinkston is still pretty tight with the mob. Not on a day-to-day basis, maybe, but tight enough they'd look after him. Maybe even pick up the pieces for him. It goes way back. You know how those guys are."

"Shit," I said.

Ricco said, "Hey, listen, if you *want* a bunch of wop button men after you, go ahead and fuck over Hinkston. Me, I think I'd try to cut a deal with him."

"That's Plan B," I said. "But I figure it will take something specific to convince Hinkston that his pal Dwight is diddling him. And I don't have zip."

Ricco shrugged.

Ed said, "Understand, though, once we can hang anything on either Hinkston or this Stapner character, we're going to pull their chains in a big hurry. That might be a problem for you later, too."

"Life is hard sometimes," I said.

"Life's a bitch," Ricco said. "Most times. You shoulda asked me; I'd have told you that right off."

CHAPTER TWENTY-SEVEN

"Thing I don't understand," Cowboy said, "is what good it does us to grab that dude. Be simpler to just blow Stapner away. He's the one causin' all the trouble."

Eight-thirty on Thursday morning. We—Cowboy, Mimi, and I—breakfasted in my office, sipping coffee and munching Danish. Maybe it didn't look like the start of a hunting expedition, but that's what it was.

Mimi grinned at me, but she spoke to Cowboy. "Rafferty wants to try a neater way first, I think."

Mimi was perched on the corner of my desk, which put her eye-level about three inches above mine and Cowboy's. We were sitting down.

Mimi is very short. She might measure in above five feet but not without her western hat. That lack of height and her round, cheery face fool people. At first glance she appears to be a teenybopper in a cowboy outfit. Except, at next glance, she's pulled an Uzi from under her coat or a small automatic from a clip inside her hat. Or a bowie knife from her boot. Or . . . Well, you get the idea.

I said to Cowboy, "Whacking Dwight Stapner wouldn't slow Hinkston down. It would probably knock him into high gear. He'd want to show he couldn't be pushed around."

Cowboy said, "Don't seem to me that anyone would miss Hinkston, either. We could do 'em both."

"Hinkston's still connected," I said. "Suppose the mob wanted to show *it* couldn't be pushed around? Where would it end?"

Cowboy smiled. "Beats me, but don't it sound like good sport?"

Mimi leaned over to pat Cowboy's shoulder. "Some other time, honey."

"Right," I said. "Look, let's just concentrate on finding the guy Dwight hired to hit Sherm. Maybe he can give us something I can take back to Hinkston."

"What perzactly?" Cowboy said.

"Anything that implicates Dwight Stapner. Maybe he hired the hitter first then fed Hinkston the story about Sherm stealing. So the timing might do it. Or maybe the hitter was involved with Dwight. Maybe he was getting a cut. Or if none of that is right, maybe Dwight said something out of line; something that will lead us to better evidence."

Cowboy sniffed. "Maybe we kin jest sit here on our butts and he'll drop by with it all written out nice and neat."

"You shitkickers do great sarcasm, I'll give you that. Remember how Hinkston waffled around when I asked him why he'd had Sherm hit in his own whorehouse? He dropped back and punted with the old 'can't get good help' line. I don't think Manny Hinkston had anything to do with organizing the hit on Sherm. I think Dwight set it up and presented it to Hinkston as a fait accompli."

"Fate-a which?"

"Fait accompli. An accomplished fact. Hinkston wouldn't wash his dirty linen in front of us, so he backed Dwight up. But there was tension there, too. I want to work on that."

"You win, boss-man," Cowboy said. "We find that library-lookin' dude and sweat him. Then what?"

"Then—assuming I'm right—we go back to Hinkston, hand him Dwight on a platter, and call it quits."

"Uh-huh. We doin' this one quiet-like or is it okay to ask around?"

I said, "Ask around. Somebody will have heard about it."

"This here Dwight fella will know we're lookin' for his hit man," Cowboy said. "Might make him spooky."

"If he does, it'll keep him off-balance. I don't see anything wrong with that."

"Okay." Cowboy drained his coffee and stood up. "We'd

best hit the street then," he said. "Get the word out, see what comes back."

"I'll be working my snitches, too," I said. "Stay in touch."

Cowboy nodded, adjusted his big hat, and ambled toward the door. Mimi hopped off my desk, waggled her fingers good-bye, and followed him. As they went, she said to Cowboy, "It might be kind of fun. Quiet, but fun."

Cowboy opened the door and grunted. He waved Mimi through ahead of him. "Gonna have to whack that sucker eventually," he said. "Betcha."

As the door closed behind them I heard Mimi say, "No bet."

I spent the rest of the morning on the phone, calling everyone who might have heard what I wanted to hear. I got mostly "don't know" answers, with a smattering of "lemme think about it; what's it worth?" and one particularly inventive report of a Louisiana voodoo princess who was sure to be the culprit. And, would you believe it, I could buy her current address for only five hundred dollars. I passed; silly me.

The phone is all right for one level of information gathering, but you can't reach everyone. Most of my street snitches, for example, had never graced the pages of Southwestern Bell. It was time to hit the bricks.

I grabbed lunch first, at a place that shouldn't be allowed to do that to an innocent burrito. They were fast, though. Gotta give them that much. By one o'clock, heartburn and all, I was hard at work.

Working the street is slow. It takes time to find people, time to repeat the spiel—again!—and time for them to jump into one category or another. By six o'clock I had acquired another dozen "don't knows," five "lemme thinks," no lies worth remembering, and sore feet.

At six-fifteen, in a watering hole not all that far from the county courthouse, I finally began to get lucky.

Ten Foot the Pole, a hard-scrabbling repo specialist, thought my description of the killer sounded familiar. "Guy with a worried look?'' Ten Foot said. ''And he carries his shoulders hunched forward just a little? That sounds like Billy Warwick.'' He pronounced it ''Warrick.''

Ten Foot's not Polish, I don't think, but he's almost six-eight and his name is something-ski, so . . .

I flagged the bartender for more beer and said, ''You're back in the will. Tell me about Billy Warwick.''

Ten Foot shrugged. ''Don't know much about him, really. I repo-ed his brother's truck four, five years ago. Billy caught me trying to get that damned truck started. I slammed the door and kept the starter cranking. I wasn't worried. Who would be? Billy looks like a wimp, right? But I remember him looking at me funny, and his eyes didn't fit with the rest of his face and that scaredy-cat way he stands. You follow me? Anyway, that stupid truck finally started, so I left.''

Ten Foot took a long gulp of beer and blew out his breath. ''Couple of weeks later I heard Billy was supposed to be a killer. Billy's not quite right in the head, according to the story, but he's sly and he's quick. I know he looks like a real dork, but . . . '' Ten Foot surrounded more beer and said, ''That's what I heard, anyway. It made me think, I'll tell you that.''

''About doing repos?''

''Aw, no, not that. Just that I should have locked the truck door, that's all.''

''Where does Warwick live, Ten Foot?''

''Dunno. The brother's place was in Irving, I think. Or maybe Grand Prairie. I'll look it up and call you tomorrow. Anyway, a while back Billy pulled a one-to-three in Huntsville. I don't remember what for, but he did his time the hard way, according to the story. Then last month I heard Billy's not only back in town, but he's looking for work.''

Ten Foot and I drank more beer, purely as a quality-control measure; then I went back to the office and my phone.

I tapped out Ed Durkee's number then put the phone down before the ringing started. Why get the DPD involved here? If I gave them Billy Warwick on a platter, they might go for Hinkston now, which would screw up Patty's conception of Sherm. Besides, I didn't know for sure that Billy Warwick was the guy we wanted. Innocent until proven guilty; right to privacy; liberte, egalite, fraternite.

Hell, I can rationalize as well as anyone.

So I didn't call Ed. I checked with my service, instead. No messages. Finally I phoned Cowboy.

"Nothing yet, Rafferty," he said. "There's one guy who's not too bad, but he ain't real good, either. He says he heard somethin' about a contract sorta like this, but I kinda think that's the Jim Beam talking."

I told him about Billy Warwick. "Run Warwick's name past your guy if you get a chance," I said. "And meet me here at noon tomorrow. By then I should have enough information on Warwick. With any luck we can do some serious hunting."

"Well, now, that sounds jest fine," Cowboy said. "I know you like all this Agent X-9 crap, but me, I just purely do like the hunting part."

CHAPTER TWENTY-EIGHT

Hilda's phone didn't answer; neither did mine. I found out why when I got home.

There was a note on my kitchen counter. Hilda had gone to Lubbock. Some rancher's antique collection was suddenly up for grabs. *Can't miss this one,* her note said. *Back on Saturday, I think. Love you.*

She'd put the time in the upper-right-hand corner of the note. Five thirty-five, it said. I had to think about it; then I remembered. At five thirty-five, I'd been giving a small-time pimp and grass dealer a hard time in an alley near the railroad yards. Hilda had probably been having more fun.

Hilda's note didn't say what kind of collection was available out in west Texas. Baroque saddles? Rococo branding irons? Ormolu spurs?

Supper was three-can surprise: chili, kidney beans, and corn this time. Afterward I watched a little television, drank a little beer, and went to bed at midnight.

Then I lay awake for a long time, wondering whether I was handling this whole Akister thing properly. Was I trying too hard to keep Patty learning the truth about Sherm? It would be tough on her, okay, but she could handle it. If she had to. Probably.

And how did that problem stack up against the problems of Becky, and perhaps Lois, with Stapner after them? You couldn't compare disillusionment with physical danger. Or—thinking then about Patty's possible reaction—could you?

Then again, maybe I was overreacting. Maybe I just wanted to see Patty Akister to repay an old debt to a long-dead teenage girl.

So what?

Goddamn it, the two hookers weren't my clients. They had a pimp. Burridge was supposed to look after them. Why was I butting in?

If I didn't, who would?

The cops, that's who. If Becky would go to the cops, that would be best. She'd get witness protection; Hinkston would be too busy to hassle Patty; a good deal all around.

Except.

Except that police involvement might cause enough public stink that Patty would find out about Sherm.

Welcome back to square one.

I dragged into the office at nine o'clock the next morning. The phone was ringing.

"I got that address for you," Ten Foot the Pole said. "Billy Warwick's brother, remember?"

"Sure. Go ahead."

"You okay? You sound funny."

"Long night. Go ahead."

Ten Foot gave me an address in Irving. "The brother's

name is Arnold,'' he said. ''I don't know if he's still there or not.''

''I owe you.''

The office coffee maker had almost finished perking when the phone rang again.

''Hey, Rafferty, man, how choo doin'? Awright?''

Diego. He hadn't been that chipper yesterday. Of course, I'd kept him talking on a street corner with his arms full of stolen car radios. Diego had looked over his shoulder a lot yesterday.

''Morning, Zorro. What's up?''

''Hey, man, I ain't usin' dat Diego el Zorro name ennymore. Guys like you, clownin' aroun', dey mess it up fo' me. It only means fox, choo know.''

''That screws up my Christmas list. No mask and sword for you.''

''Dere! See! Dat's wha' I mean, man. But wha' choo t'ink of dis? Diego el Lobo. Diego the wolf. Good, huh?''

''Not too original.''

''Well, is only a thought. Enny way, 'bout dat t'ing you say yesterday. Mebbe I got news for choo.''

''Good.''

''Only, ah . . . Hey, man, dere's this little t'ing 'bout da money, choo know.''

''You'll get it, Diego. You know that. Why do we go through this every time?''

''Yeah, well . . . aw righ', since it's choo, Rafferty, dat's okay. Choo my main man, righ'?''

''My bullshit alarm is going off here, Diego. I think I'll hang up now.''

''No, is okay, man! Here's da story. Dis guy I know, he say dere was a Anglo dude askin' around 'bout where he could hire a hitter, righ'? A really big dude, dis guy says, but he doan know his name.''

''Big, about six-four? Heavy beard, looks like he has to shave two or three times a day?''

''Could be, man, I doan know. Dat sounds right, though.''

''I think I know who that is. Your buddy hear who this guy eventually hired?''

"Naw. Nuttin' 'bout dat."

"Could he have hired Billy Warwick?"

"Naw, man. Dat Warwick, he's in the slammer."

"Hell he is. He's been out for a month, at least."

"No kiddin'?"

"No kidding. Hey, Diego, what's the Spanish for kitten?"

"Is *gatito*, man. Why?"

"Diego el Gatito," I said. "You gotta admit, that has a ring to it."

"Aw, c'mon, man."

"I'll get your money to you." I hung up on Diego and sat back with a cup of fresh coffee, beginning to feel good about the day. Always did like Fridays, and this looked like a good one. Ten Foot and Diego had come through for me.

Some you win.

I still had to find Billy Warwick, though. No sweat. The phone book had a number for Arnold Warwick in Irving. I called the number.

A woman answered. "Hello?" She managed to get a cheery country twang into the single word.

I said, "Hi. Billy there?"

All the cheer drained out of her voice. "No, he is not here. And he won't be back, either, not as long I have anything to say about it." The phone rattled loudly then went dead.

Some you lose.

I called the Texas State Parole offices in Dallas—both of them—and said I was a Huntsville prison official named Hackstanding.

No one knew anything about a Warwick, William, paroled out of Huntsville in the last six months. They seemed a little worried about that.

Then I called Huntsville and pretended to be a parole officer named Hackstanding. The guy in Huntsville wasn't worried at all.

"Haw!" he said. "You goddamn bleeding hearts don't get to play with that one. Son of a bitch Warwick didn't get paroled. He served his whole sentence, every goddamn day of it."

"Got an address for him?" I said.

He thought that was very funny. The laugh turned into a bad smoker's cough. When he could talk again, he wheezed, "Anything you got for Warwick, you send it here. He'll be back."

Some get rained out.

Okay, so where do we go from here? Warwick was fresh from the slammer; he wouldn't have a car yet. Well, he might have one, probably did, but the paperwork wouldn't have caught up yet. There was no use trying to track him down that way.

He'd be bunking in with someone or living in a rented room. No records to search there, either.

A job? Warwick's trade didn't deal with W-2s or Social Security or workman's compensation or group insurance policies or any other back-door way I could locate him.

Wait a minute, he might have a normal job. As a cover, maybe, or just because job opportunities for small-time hit men don't come along every day. And they don't pay all that well when they do. If Warwick had a job, a real job, he'd be popping up on the computers already.

All right, assume he has a legit job. Where should I start looking? Social Security and the IRS were Washington-based; very tough to get information from. Supposedly you can't get information about taxes or Social Security. There are guys who do, of course, but I'm not one of them. Damn it.

Workman's comp was a possibility, though. Group insurance, too, although that meant blind calls. Lots of blind calls. Do you have any idea how many insurance companies operate in Texas?

There was a guy I'd used before who could dig up workman's comp information. I called him, but he wasn't too happy. For some reason it was harder to start with the individual's name and come up with the employer than it was to start with the employer's name and come up with the individual. I don't know why; computers are too high-tech for me.

"Okay, okay, I can do it," Ray said. "I'll just take longer, that's all. What's the full name?"

"Warwick. Billy Warwick, so I guess that's William."

"You *guess* it's William? Is it William something Warwick or something William Warwick? And, hey, it could really be Billy, couldn't it? I mean, some Billys aren't Williams."

"I don't know. Can't you try them all?"

"Forget it." Ray hung up.

Like I said, some get rained out.

Ten minutes later I got a call from another snitch I'd contacted the day before. Willie's girlfriend, who did a little hooking from time to time, had been warned off working for one of Hinkston's houses. Too dangerous, she'd been told. Big changes coming, and no telling which of the bosses would still be around next month.

Interesting.

Cowboy and Mimi bounced into the office at noon, raring to go.

"Let's git him," Cowboy said.

"Small problem," I said. "I haven't worked out exactly where he is, yet."

Cowboy's seamed face clouded; Mimi grinned up at us.

"It won't take long," I said. "Probably. Let's go check out his brother's house."

"Hope we ain't wasting our time," Cowboy grumbled. "We do thumpin' and shootin', things like that. I purely hate this detecting stuff."

"Did I forget to tell you where we're going? Warwick's brother is a biker gang leader. They'll be guarding their amphetamine lab, I suppose. Be lots of automatic weapons, and we'll be outnumbered, but . . ."

Cowboy shook his head sadly. "You're funning me, Rafferty. I know that. But, doggone it, for jest a second there, you had my hopes up."

CHAPTER TWENTY-NINE

The Irving address belonged to a small frame house in the middle of its block. It was a stolid working-class neighborhood. Nobody here was hurting badly, but nobody was getting rich, either. This was pickup truck, gimme cap, and *Wrestlemania* country.

A four- or five-year-old Ford was parked in the driveway of the Warwick house. There was no one in the front yard; what I could see of the back yard was empty, too.

"Check out ole Big Eyes over there," Cowboy said. "That sucker's been staring ever since you turned onto this here street."

"Big Eyes" was a potbellied man in his sixties who was watering a lawn across the street and three doors up from Warwick's house.

I wheeled the Mustang into the curb in front of the watering man's house. "Seize available opportunities to interrogate potential informants," I said. "That was the theme of a riveting editorial in last month's *Private Investigator's Digest.*"

Mimi, in the back seat, giggled. Cowboy groaned. "Lord-a-mercy," he said.

"Come on, Cowboy," I said. "I'll show you how this works."

The man with the hose watched us suspiciously as we got

out of the car and walked toward him. He had a good face for suspicion; his cheeks were round, like his belly, but his eyes were small and deep-seated. I had thought he was bald, but when we got close I saw he had very short gray hair. He didn't have a nozzle on the hose; he held his thumb over the end to make a spray.

"Afternoon, sir," I said, and showed him a card in my wallet that says I'm a field agent for the Federal Investigative Agency, whatever that is. "Try not to look obvious, sir. We're undercover today."

"Yeah?" he said, looked from Cowboy to me. There was still suspicion in his little eyes, but there was more curiosity. He took a step closer to us, and he held the hose down and off to one side. He stopped spraying.

"Routine field survey, sir," I said. I dug my notebook out of my hip pocket and flipped it open. "Agent Johannsen and I have a few questions about, ah, Arnold Warwick."

"Arnie? Why? What's up with Arnie?"

"No problem, sir," I said. "Purely routine. How long has Warwick lived over there?"

"How long? Hell, I don't know. Eight years? Maybe nine. But, listen, why—" The force of the water from the man's hose had begun to dig a hole in his lawn.

"Would you say Warwick is a pretty normal fellow? Lives with his wife, does he?"

"Yeah, that's right. Corinne's her name. And one kid. But—"

"Anyone else living in the household, as far as you know?" I gave him a serious look. "We check for unusual domestic situations, alternative lifestyles, things like that."

The old man looked confused. "Naw, just Arnie, Corinne, and the kid. Nobody else. Oh, well, his brother was there for a couple of days recently. Maybe it was a week, but I don't see . . ." He still hadn't shifted his hose. A fair-sized puddle had formed, but he didn't seem to notice.

I flipped another notebook page. "Brother, brother . . . Yessss, that fits with what I have here. Where did Warwick say his brother went after that visit?"

"He didn't say." Then he noticed the muddy puddle and

jerked the hose away. "Aw, shit, look what you made me do. What the hell is all this about, anyway?"

"Routine, sir. What can you tell me—"

He lashed the hose from side to side so the water wouldn't dig another hole. "Wait a minute now. I ain't saying any more until you tell me what's going on! What did Arnie do? Uh, I mean, what's he supposed to have done?"

"It's confid—ah, well, I suppose I can tell you. He's in line for a promotion at work, and there are national security implications. Government contracts, classified material. You understand, I'm sure."

"*Security?* Arnie?" He shook his head and whipped the hose in the same rhythm. "You're outta your mind, pal. Arnie Warwick sells tires, for crying out loud. What's that got to do with national security?"

"Tires?" I said. "No, sir, Arnold Warwick is a lab technician for Atomic Chemical and Research. You must be mistaken."

"You dummies!" His little eyes glinted. "Your federal government at work, huh. When I think of the money you dickheads waste . . . You got the wrong Arnold Warwick, pal. Atomic research, my butt. Go out to Indian Head and see for yourself. Shit!"

"Well, we'll certainly investigate this, sir. Ah, Indian Head?"

The old man stared at the soggy patch on his lawn. "Yeah. Indian Head Tires. Out on Irving Boulevard. Aw, damn it. See what you made me do?"

"Thanks for your cooperation, sir," I said. "Let's go, Agent Johannsen."

The old man flapped a weary hand at us and walked toward his house, still lashing the hose rapidly from side to side. He should have used a nozzle.

As we got into the car, Cowboy muttered, "Agent Johannsen? You think I look like a goddamn Viking?"

"Viking?" Mimi said. "What's going on?"

"You don't want to know," Cowboy said. "Now what?"

"Now we talk to the brother."

* * *

Indian Head Tire-Rama was a smallish place compared to some of the other tire dealers on Irving Boulevard. There was room for half-a-dozen cars to park in front, a narrow drive to the back, where they fitted the tires, and a showroom swathed in plate glass.

"I ain't gonna go in there with you," Cowboy said. "Next thing you'll be calling me Agent Bernstein or O'Rourke or something."

"Suit yourself." I left Cowboy and Mimi wandering around outside and opened the showroom door. Inside there were new tires on stands so you could admire the knobby treads. Three people sat in chairs in a corner, reading old magazines, looking bored. There was a coffee machine nearby.

At the back of the showroom there was a counter. Behind the counter, windows and a glass-paneled door looked out onto the bays where two cars were jacked up, having new tires mounted.

A man in his late twenties wearing blue coveralls thumbed through a catalog on the counter. He found what he wanted, stuck his finger on the entry, and repeated it to himself, concentrating. Then he saw me and said, "Help you?"

"Arnold Warwick? Is he in?"

"In the back," he said. "He'll be out in a minute." He looked at the catalog entry under his thumb again, nodded, and went out the door to the working area.

I waited. In the working bay closest to the windows, another man in coveralls squatted and used an air wrench to tighten the wheel nuts on a yellow Taurus. A desk jockey watched him work. The supervisor was mid-thirties, prematurely balding, with a clipboard and a worried expression. He peered at the wheel-tightening process like he'd never seen it done before.

The guy who'd memorized the catalog number apparently called out to the man with the clipboard. Clipboard looked in at me and made a vague "be with you in a minute" gesture.

Then the mechanic with the air wrench stood up and half turned toward me. It was Billy Warwick. Hot damn!

Billy Warwick in mechanic's overalls looked different, but there was no doubt it was him. Same defensive stance; same hangdog look. Now he looked like he was ashamed of the air wrench he held.

One of the other mechanics saw me coming through the door and called out, "Sorry, sir. Customer's aren't—"

Warwick looked up and threw the air wrench at me in almost the same motion. His diffident appearance was misleading. He was fast.

I ducked; the hose connected to the air wrench stopped it short of me, anyway, and then I was a full fifteen steps behind Warwick.

As he went out the back of the working bay and turned left, Mimi and Cowboy ran past the opening, close on his heels.

Ducking around the Taurus, I almost stumbled over a young man working at the back wheel. We did that *this way, no, that way, no, no, this way* dance you see on crowded sidewalks, then I was around him, out into the back lot, and where the hell was Billy Warwick?

There was a high wire fence around the lot with a stack of wooden pallets on the far side of the back fence on what appeared to be a warehouse site. Cowboy was halfway between me and that fence, walking back toward me. He brushed his hands together and smiled. "Let's go, bossman."

"Where is he?"

"No sweat. Let's go."

The mechanics and the man with the clipboard caught up with us then. They wanted to know what was going on, too. Especially the guy with the clipboard.

"Now listen!" he said. "You can't come in and . . ."

Cowboy led the way up the narrow lane, back toward the front of the building and the parked Mustang.

"I'll call the police," the tire man shouted, skipping beside us. Then he turned on the small crowd of mechanics following. "Go back to work, everybody, I'll handle this."

When they'd started back he ran to catch up with us again. "I'm serious," he said. "I will call the police. Right now."

"Go ahead, Arnold," I guessed.

"How did you . . . Wait a minute, I don't . . ."

Cowboy and I got into the Mustang. It started on only the second try. As I backed out of the slot, Arnold Warwick trotted over and crouched beside the car.

"What has Billy done now?" he said. "Look, you've got to tell me what—"

"Hang a right," Cowboy said.

I did. As I turned out of the Indian Head Tire-Rama, Arnold screamed something unintelligible and threw his clipboard. It clunked against the trunk lid then dropped off onto the road. When I looked in the rearview mirror, Arnold was picking it up. He stared at us leaving him, then he turned away. His shoulders were almost as rounded as Billy's.

"Turn right here, I think," Cowboy said.

A block later we turned right again. About a hundred yards along, Cowboy pointed. "Down there, maybe."

I turned in. We drove down another narrow strip of concrete, this time beside a large, apparently empty metal building. The driveway opened up behind the building. I recognized the stack of pallets. We were behind the Tire-Rama.

Next to the pallets Billy Warwick lay facedown on the concrete. He had his fingers laced behind the back of his neck. Mimi stood well clear of his feet with a 9-mm Beretta aimed at the back of his head.

"Hi, guys," she said.

CHAPTER THIRTY

Before we let Billy Warwick stand up, Cowboy went through the pockets of his baggy overalls. Nothing. Warwick came up sullenly. "You guys cops or what?" he said.

He started to lower his arms, then Mimi murmured, "Unh uh," and he raised them again.

"Hell, no, we're not cops," I said. "Check under those coveralls, Cowboy. You could hide a rocket launcher in there."

Well, maybe not a rocket launcher, but there was a Stanley razor knife in one hip pocket of the jeans Warwick wore under his coveralls. And a three-inch length of galvanized pipe in another pocket.

"Cheaper than a roll of quarters, eh, Billy? You can put your arms down now."

With his hands down Warwick's shoulders rounded into his normal slouch. Behind him Mimi slipped her Beretta beneath her jacket.

Warwick looked worried. He said, "If you're not cops, who are you?"

"Later," I said. I opened the trunk of the Mustang and pointed at it. "Get in."

Warwick took a half-step toward the Mustang then pivoted on the ball of his right foot, around Mimi. He lunged for the driveway and the open street beyond.

As he took the third step Mimi side-kicked his left knee. He went down in a tumbling, cursing heap.

"Fool," she said to him. "Get into the trunk, like he said."

That time Warwick got into the trunk.

I took Warwick to my house. Cowboy wanted to go the other way, out beyond the airport into the countryside. He said there were plenty of open spaces in the fresh air where we could talk to Warwick. I said there were plenty of closed-in spaces in the city where we could do the same thing. One of the differences between country boys and city boys, I guess.

Home on Palm Lane, I wrestled with the clumsy garage door until I got it open, then drove the Mustang inside, closed the door, and finally let Warwick out of the trunk. Palm Lane was not the sort of neighborhood where you paraded your kidnap victims openly.

Warwick had had time to think on the drive across town. He came out of the trunk on a soapbox. "You'll be sorry for this," he ranted. "Criminal assault. Kidnapping. I was minding my own business. . . . Hurt my leg something terrible . . . Call police . . . Sue you . . ." There was a lot more but that pretty well sums it up.

I used a come-along hold to move Warwick into the house then handcuffed him to a kitchen chair. I found a six-pack of Bud in the refrigerator, handed cans around to Cowboy and Mimi, then sat down at the table with Warwick. Mimi perched on the kitchen counter; Cowboy leaned against the counter beside her.

"Now, Billy," I said, "let us begin with the facts. You whacked Sherm Akister for—"

"Who, me? I don't know nothing about—"

"You whacked Sherm Akister. You passed us on the way out of the hooker's apartment, remember? Don't bullshit me, Billy. It only makes the day longer than it has to be."

Warwick looked around the room and wet his lips. He leaned against the handcuffs, gingerly at first, then putting all this strength into it. The chair didn't break, which surprised me a little bit. Finally Warwick subsided, sweating some then, and he said, "If you're not cops, who are you?"

"Here's the way it lays out," I said. "Dwight Stapner hired you to take out a man—Sherm—in a small-time whorehouse. He might have told you Sherm was a thief; he might not. In any case, you made the hit and, I assume, got paid. Now Dwight wants at least one, maybe both, hookers hit. You helped him try once, but ended up in a store window."

Warwick stared at me. "Yeah, well, that's crap. But say, just say, some guy really did all that. What's it to you?"

"Dwight's not the boss; Dwight is the thief." I gave Warwick a brief, but accurate, version of my theory. "What's important is when Dwight hired you. And what he said when he did."

"That's not important to me," Warwick said. "No way."

"Did I mention yet that Hinkston is mob-connected? And the mob isn't reasonable and understanding like I am. If they tumble to Dwight's scam, they'll be after everyone involved. Do you really think they'll say, 'Aw, let's give good old Billy a break. He didn't know what was going on.' " I tried for a foreboding stare. "I don't think they'll say that."

Warwick wet his lips again and blinked. "How do I know you're not mob?"

"You don't."

"Or cops," he said.

"You don't. And there's even another angle to this, Billy. Suppose you don't do anything to help clear this up. Then, once the hooker's out of the way, why would Dwight want you around? You might be next."

Billy huffed. "I could take that guy Dwight."

I made a show of turning and looking at Mimi, who'd taken Billy. Twice. She waggled her fingers at me and grinned.

Billy grunted and made a face. "What'll you pay me?"

"One handcuff key. Take it or leave it."

"I can go afterward? No shit?"

"No shit."

"Why should I believe that?"

"What have you got to lose?"

Warwick made an odd sucking sound with his lip for ten or fifteen seconds, then he sighed. "All right," he said. "I don't want to get into no trouble with the mob. What do you want to know, just about this guy Dwight and all?"

"Talk to me, Billy. Whisper in my shell-like ear."

"Yeah, well, all he told me was they had a problem with a money guy. He was stealing, like you said, and Dwight wanted him taken out."

"What about the hooker?"

Billy Warwick shook his head emphatically. "Nobody said anything about a girl then. Just the guy."

"Exactly who hired you?"

"Dwight, like you said. He's the only one I ever saw. All the rest of this stuff is news to me."

"When did he hire you?"

Warwick said, "Four, five weeks ago, something like that."

"What took you so long?"

"Hey, that wasn't me dragging my feet. He got me all set to go then told me to wait. Not yet, he kept saying, I'll let you know. It was a real pain."

"You didn't like the wait, Billy? You get off on killing people?"

"Naw, I needed the money, that's all."

"How did Dwight find you?"

"Oh, well, I got out of Huntsville about, what, eight weeks ago now. Moved in with my brother. I put out the word on the street I was back. Looking for work, you know. And this Dwight character was looking for a hard man, so . . . we got together. You know how it is."

"And that was five weeks ago?"

"Oh, yeah, something like that. But after I agreed to do it, then Dwight started jerking me around. Not yet, not yet, he said. I was broke, right? I borrowed some money from my brother but that didn't sit too good with this bitch of a wife he's got." He jerked his arms, rattled the handcuffs. "Any chance of . . . ?"

"Later, maybe. Keep talking."

"Well, like I say, I was broke, and Dwight's job didn't

look like it was ever gonna happen. I got one other job, but . . . See, I boosted a car for this guy, but I kind of screwed up. Arnie's wife saw the car and knew right off what had happened. Threw me out of the house. Her own brother-in-law. The bitch.''

After a moment he sniffed and went on. ''Well, then I was really up against it. Arnie loaned me another couple hundred and got me a job down at the tire place. It's the shits, but I got to have some money coming in. On my own, there's rent and food, all that stuff. It's not easy.''

''When did Dwight finally say he wanted the job done?''

''The day I did it. What was that, a week ago yesterday, right? He called me at work that Thursday morning and said to do it that night.''

Sherm had made the rounds of Hinkston's shonky businesses on Wednesday night, asking what Becky Chalmers had called ''the right questions this time.'' Thursday morning, Dwight wanted Sherm dead. Gotcha, Dwight.

''What about the girl?'' I asked Billy. ''When did Dwight tell you he wanted the girl hit, too?''

''Oh, that wasn't until this Monday. He called me at work again. See, I decided to keep that tire job for a while, 'cause it might look funny if I quit too soon. Cops get suspicious of us ex-cons. It ain't fair.''

Billy's story didn't prove Dwight was working behind Hinkston's back, but it opened up the strong possibility. Manny Hinkston would have to check it out. He was a crazy son of a bitch, but I was fairly sure he was also a suspicious son of a bitch.

''Billy, all you have to do is tell that one more time, to Hinkston, then I'll drive you home.''

''Hey, you didn't say anything about that!''

''Must have slipped my mind.''

Warwick groaned and shook his head. I grinned at him. ''You don't have anything better to do for the next hour or so.''

Hour or so, hell, I thought. Billy Warwick didn't have anything better to do for the rest of his life.

I phoned Hinkston Bargain Furniture and asked for Manny. It took a long time, but he finally came on the line.

"Hey, Rafferty, what's the fucking problem now? I'm a busy man here." There was an unusual soft sound; I could imagine him slapping himself in the mouth with a cigarette.

"Manny, there's more to this Sherm and Becky Chalmers fiasco than you think. I want to bring a guy over to talk to you."

"Feeass-what? What the fuck are you talking about?"

"This guy knows things you want to hear, Manny. Trust me. We'll be there in half an hour."

"Wait a minute." Hinkston partially covered the phone. I could hear voices and, once, a coughing fit, but I couldn't tell what was being said.

Then he was back. "I told you, I'm busy, goddamn it. Make it, ah, eight o'clock. And it better be good, you hear me? I ain't got time for this kinda shit."

"Okay. Eight o'clock. There will be three of us."

Hinkston hung up without saying anything.

I hung up, too, and said, "If Shirley MacLaine is right about past lives, that jerk used to be a warthog."

CHAPTER THIRTY-ONE

Fifteen minutes after I set up the appointment with Hinkston, the phone rang. I hoped it was Hilda, back from Lubbock a day early.

It wasn't.

"I'm out three days' earnings because two of my ladies are sitting on their fuzzy little money-makers. How're you doing?" Roosevelt Burridge's voice was deep and smooth.

"Funny you should mention that," I said. "The fix is

almost in. Keep the girls tucked away tonight, but by tomorrow . . . I'll let you know when the heat's off. Where?''

"Maybe I better call you," Burridge said. "I hope you're right, Rafferty. Not working's bad for the ladies. They start getting ideas.''

"Call me tomorrow.''

"Tomorrow." He hung up.

At six o'clock I rummaged around to see what was available for supper. "Bacon and eggs?" I said. "Spam sandwiches? Sardines?''

"Ribs," Cowboy said. "Me and Mimi'll go get 'em.''

Billy Warwick looked from Cowboy to me. "Yeah, ribs," he said. "I'll go for ribs.''

"Leave him cuffed till we git back," Mimi said. "He's a speedy little weasel.''

"Even so," Billy said, "I still want the ribs.''

While they were gone I realized I hadn't talked to Patty Akister for two days, since Sherm's funeral. I called her. She answered on the third ring.

"It's Rafferty, Patty. How are you?''

"I'm fine, thank you very much." She sounded a little tentative, not too bad.

I said, "I thought I'd just, ah, see how you're doing.''

"Thank you," she said again. "I've been thinking. Shouldn't I have heard from the government by now? Because, you see, I'm afraid that Sherm won't get the recognition he deserves. And . . . ''

I fumbled around with that one for a while and finally convinced her, I hoped, that espionage agents were usually given awards within the agency but not publicly. Security and all that.

"But shouldn't they have contacted me?''

"Give it time, Patty. Ah, did you get the insurance money?''

Who, me? Change the subject?

"Yes, the check came today." She said the payout would hold her for a while but not indefinitely, so she'd have to think about going back to work. Maybe her old job was still available. She didn't like that job particularly, but she wanted to stay busy, and the money would be helpful.

I felt uneasy chatting with Patty about those things. I didn't know whether she wanted me to tell her she was doing the right thing, tell her she was doing the wrong thing, suggest something else, or simply murmur sympathetically.

I settled for the murmur, and I wished Hilda was there. She's good at that stuff.

I got off the phone when Cowboy and Mimi came back with the food. We moved the table to box Billy into a corner and let him eat without the cuffs. What the hell, if he could get away by going over all three of us, he deserved it.

Billy didn't try anything, though. He seemed resigned to the trip to Hinkston's. He gnawed his ribs happily, ate more beans than anyone else, and claimed that, overall, the meal compared favorably to Huntsville mess-hall food.

At seven-fifteen we left the house. Billy promised to be good. "You don't need the cuffs," he said. "Those things are creepy. They remind me of cops."

"Cuff him," Cowboy and Mimi said in chorus. I had already started to do so. We put him in the back seat with Mimi.

We went downtown first and dropped Mimi at their parked pickup. I gave her my front-door key. "We'll be about an hour probably. Maybe a little more. Then I'll bring Cowboy home before I take Billy back to Irving."

"See ya," Mimi said, and scrambled up into the truck. When you're that short, a pickup truck must seem like a metal wall.

"Don't you worry about her?" Billy asked Cowboy. "I mean, hey, she's gonna drive back all alone, at night. There's some bad dudes around."

Cowboy looked at him like he had three heads. "Are you funnin' me?"

I said, "You bet on the muggers, Billy. I'll take Mimi, and you can name the stakes."

He nodded. "Yeah, okay, I see what you guys mean."

For the run out to Garland Road and Hinkston's furniture store I made Billy sit in the passenger seat with Cowboy in the rear. The Mustang's back seat wasn't big enough for both of them, and I didn't want Billy behind me, alone. Like so many of my decisions, that one drew a mixed response. Cowboy grumbled about the shortage of legroom; Billy thought he was coming up in the world.

They took us at a stoplight two blocks short of the furniture store. I had stopped behind a nondescript van on the red. But then the van didn't move out when the light changed. Uh-oh.

I grabbed for reverse and floored it. The Mustang lurched back about six inches then crunched into a big Ford station wagon planted rock-solid behind us.

"Ambush!" I yelled.

It was already too late. Another car—a Buick, I think—was hard against my door now. A fat man with a biker's hairy face grinned at me over a double-barreled shotgun aimed at my throat.

"Shit!" Billy said. "What the—"

There was another biker type in the Buick with another shotgun aimed into the back seat of the Mustang. Behind me Cowboy said, "Well, goddamn."

The back doors of the van ahead opened. Another man, crouched inside, covered us with an automatic weapon I didn't recognize. Bigger than an Uzi or MAC, smaller than an M-16. A Steyr, maybe.

The Mustang's passenger door jerked open. Billy screamed and threw himself toward my side of the car. Big hands reached in and clawed at him, dragged him out. As he went Billy tried to hook the handcuff chain over the gearshift lever. He missed; I felt sick to my stomach.

Another man appeared. He crouched by the Mustang's right front wheel. There was the smallest of shakes, then that corner of the car dropped as the tire went flat.

They hustled Billy around the Mustang toward the gaping doors of the van. Billy fought them; they held his upper arms. Billy dropped to his knees by the van's rear bumper. He yelled something, I think. His mouth was open wide and the cords on his neck stood out like he was yelling.

I couldn't hear him, not with the slow, heavy thud of my pulse in my ears. I snapped a look at the biker covering me from the Buick; his grin widened, and he shook his head.

In front Billy was still on his knees, writhing and fighting, handicapped by the handcuffs. One of the men holding him pulled out a flat black automatic pistol and shot Billy once in the back of the neck. Billy went down like a puppet with the strings cut, flopped out of sight in front of the Mustang.

"Easy, boss," I heard Cowboy say from far away. "This un's theirs. Next time it's our turn."

Billy's killer shoved the pistol back into his belt, bent down, and set himself like a weightlifter at the heavy bar. He jerked, came up with Billy's body held by the shirt and belt, then threw it into the van at the feet of the man with the automatic weapon. He and his pal followed the body in, the doors closed, and the van lurched away.

Beside me the Buick's tires squalled. It left, too, scraping along the Mustang as it pulled away.

The Ford wagon backed away from my rear bumper, went around us, and limped away, trailing steam and strange noises.

A white Pontiac going the other way had almost stopped. The driver peered at us curiously as the Pontiac crawled along, then his head turned and he accelerated away.

Lights came up behind, then swerved around the Mustang. A cab. Its horn blared a reprimand for blocking the street.

Cowboy sighed. "Those fellas were good, Rafferty. You recognize 'em?"

"No."

The street was returning to normal. Opposing traffic flowed smoothly. On this side cars pulled out around us. We were just a broken-down car, that's all. No big deal.

Hey, didn't you see that? They dragged that guy out and shot him!

Get out! C'mon, seriously, which movie you wanna see?

Cowboy prodded the back of my seat. "Let's git that tire changed."

"I'm screwed now," I said. "Without Warwick I can't convince Hinkston about Dwight."

Cowboy pushed his way out of the back seat. "Gotta try, though. Gimme your trunk key."

That son-of-a-bitch Dwight smirked at us. That was the worst part. He smirked.

Cowboy and I stood at the bottom of the staircase leading up to Hinkston's offices; Dwight and the blond goon stood at the top, behind Manny Hinkston. And Dwight smirked while Manny ranted.

"What the fuck, huh? What's the matter with you? Big deal phone call. 'Manny, I gotta talk to you. Manny, a guy has something to tell you.' So where is this guy? What's he got to tell me? Huh, what?" He threw away the cigarette stub he was holding and snapped his fingers. The blond hulk held out a pack for Manny then lighted his new cigarette. Manny blew out smoke and scowled at us. "Come on, you dumb fucks. What's going on here?"

The store was closed; most of the showroom was dark. One bank of overhead lights had been left on to light up the staircase, with us at the bottom and Hinkston's merry men at the top.

I took a deep breath. "Watch your back, Manny. You—"

"Watch my back? You're telling me to watch my fucking back? I don't need you to tell me—Look, you got something to say, say it."

Cowboy muttered, "Forgit it, boss-man."

Dwight smirked.

"One thing, Manny," I said. "Our deal about leaving Sherm's wife alone still stands, right?"

Hinkston frowned and slapped himself with his cigarette. "Why not? What's the big . . . Hey, Rafferty, who the fuck you think you are, bugging me about a pissant little thing like that? I told you we had a deal. And I told you tonight I was busy." He sucked on the smoke again then waved his hand at us. "Get outa here."

Hinkston turned and went into the office loft.

Dwight smirked. "You heard him," he said. "Piss off."

We left. Outside, beside the Mustang, Cowboy stopped

and turned back toward Hinkston's darkened store. He took off his western hat, slapped it against his leg, and carefully replaced it. "I didn't feel too bad when we got Warwick took away from us. I didn't like it, but they was good, and they caught us fair and square."

"I felt bad," I said.

"But now," Cowboy said, "now I'm madder'n hell. That big sucker was laughing at us, Rafferty. Did you see him laughing?"

"I saw him."

"He laughed at us. That don't set well with me. That don't set well at all. I want him."

"Cowboy, the problem hasn't changed. I have to discredit Dwight, not whack him."

Cowboy let out a loud breath. "So you tell me. But one of these days you'll see that it ain't gonna work that way. Not with that old boy." Cowboy pointed a bony finger at me over the top of the Mustang. "And when the time comes, he's mine, Rafferty. Don't forgit. That sucker is mine."

We left then and drove back to my house, where we had to tell Mimi what had happened to us. That was hard.

And Hilda wasn't there, so I couldn't tell her what had happened to us. That was hard, too.

I'm not sure exactly which was the hardest.

CHAPTER THIRTY-TWO

"I wish I didn't know about the things you do," Hilda said. "Sometimes, anyway. But then again, it might be worse not knowing."

"They weren't after me," I said. "They wanted Billy

Warwick; they got him. Without much difficulty, goddamn it.''

It was Saturday night. Hilda had returned from the wilds of Lubbock, bright-eyed with fierce glee, burdened with treasures. We were celebrating, sprawled on her bed, sipping chardonnay and beer. We were both naked. Not for the first time I noticed that naked looked better on Hilda than it did on me.

Hilda said, ''And you think Warwick's kidnap, his murder, was organized by this creature Dwight so his boss wouldn't find out about him.''

''Right. Dwight has been stealing from Hinkston for a while, I think. I don't know the details. I don't know how, or how long, or how much, but it must be a nice chunk of change. Hinkston is not a guy from whom you steal a little bit. If you're going to steal, you steal a whole lot. That's the only way to make the return match the risk.''

''Did you say 'from whom'?'' Hilda said. ''Have you become civilized when I wasn't looking?''

''I think they're putting something in the water now. Anyway, Dwight has been stealing from Hinkston and covering it up, okay? So one day Hinkston started zinging Sherm Akister, acting like he thought *Sherm* was stealing. I don't know how that happened. Maybe Hinkston really did find out about a small part of Dwight's action, but he got the wrong guy. Maybe—this would be real sneaky if he did it this way—maybe Dwight deliberately let Hinkston see a little cash going missing. As misdirection, right? Then Hinkston would worry about Sherm stealing nickels, while Dwight was shoveling crisp green fifties out the back door. That's kind of cute, actually.''

Hilda finger-combed her tangled hair. ''They why did he have Sherm killed?''

''I'm not sure. Dwight had Billy Warwick primed and ready to go for weeks, so there are two possibilities. One: Dwight had Billy ready just in case, not to be used unless Hinkston got suspicious. When that happened, Dwight was the efficient right-hand man. *Okay, boss. I found out who did that, and he's history*. Two: Dwight planned to implicate and execute Sherm from the beginning. *Took care of that little problem, boss. See how loyal I am?*

"It doesn't really matter which of those things happened, does it?" Hilda said. "Not to Sherm. Or to Patty."

"Nope. Either way, Sherm never had a chance. The poor klutz thought he could clear himself with Hinkston, but Dwight was way ahead of him." I thought about what I'd just said, then added, "Like Dwight was way ahead of me when I tried to do the same thing."

"Now, now," Hilda said, "don't blame yourself. That man Warwick was a hired killer, after all. Which reminds me. I'm surprised you were going to let him go. I guess I thought you'd want to, ah . . ."

"Avenge Sherm?" I said. "Why? Sherm knew what he was getting into, doing dirty work for Hinkston. You can't play with rattlesnakes, get bitten, then claim it's a big surprise." I got another beer from the bedside ice bucket. "But Patty didn't know any of that. It wasn't her fault. Besides, 'avenging' Sherm wouldn't do him any good; if I can keep Sherm's background from Patty, that helps her."

Hilda said, "I've heard of inventive rationalization, but . . ."

"It makes sense to me."

After a moment Hilda said, "So you don't think Hinkston knows about Billy Warwick?"

"Oh, well, he knows that Billy killed Sherm, and he may even know his name. But I bet Hinkston doesn't know Billy is dead or that Billy was the guy coming with me last night. Damn, but I feel stupid. I should have known Dwight would pull something last night. I should have seen it coming, Hil."

"Blaming yourself won't help. Have you told the police yet?"

"Ah, not yet."

"Are you going to?"

"I doubt it. I didn't tell them about Warwick when he was alive; how can I tell them now?"

Hilda shook her head. "Other men have problems like getting a pay raise or crabgrass. Your problems are . . . Well, all right, then. What about the prostitute, Becky, and her friend? Are they still in danger?"

"More than ever, I'd say. Dwight must feel pretty good

now. He got rid of Warwick; if he takes out one or both of the hookers, he's eliminated everyone who was there that night.''

''Their pimp is hiding them, though, isn't he?''

I told Hilda about Burridge's phone call the night before and how I'd assured him everything would be all right by today. ''Burridge called again this morning. He sounded pretty chipper; said he was anxious to get the girls back to work. I told him about last night. That was easier than taking out my own appendix with a rusty screwdriver, I guess. Not much, but a little bit.'' I drank some beer. ''Burridge won't keep them hidden much longer. He's tired of all this. In another day or two he's going to shove them out onto the street.''

''Whereupon they will be killed.''

I nodded. ''Got it in one, babe.''

Hilda bounced around to face me. As the waterbed wobbles died away, she said, ''Wait a minute. You and Cowboy were at that apartment that night. If this man Dwight is so bloodthirsty, why didn't he do anything to you two last night?''

''He couldn't,'' I said. ''Hinkston was waiting for us to show up at eight o'clock. If we'd turned up dead instead, Hinkston would ask himself why. That would draw attention to Dwight not divert it.''

''I wish I felt you were as safe as you do. As safe as . . . you know what I mean.''

''Understood. Don't forget, though, that the dastardly forces of evil are not dealing with your average thug here. I'm, uh, well-known and, er, renowned for . . .'' I stopped, sipped beer, and finally said, ''That was miserable last night, Hil. I can't even concoct my usual bullshit when I remember sitting there in the car letting them take Billy Warwick away.''

''Do you think he knew what was going to happen?''

I remembered Billy's face when they dragged him out of the car. ''He knew,'' I said.

We sat quietly for a while, then Hilda said, ''You do have a problem with this case, don't you?''

''Well, let's see. My client is a naive widow of a dead bagman, but she thinks he was a heroic secret agent. There are also one or two hookers who would like to stay alive, and it's difficult to find fault with that goal. Among the black hats, we have an unstable hood—Hinkston—who says he'll be nice, but he acts like Vlad the Impaler with a stomach-ache. And then there's Dwight, who definitely will not be nice, no matter what he says. Oh, yeah, and on the sidelines we have the cops, who would be involved by now except that I've withheld most of the evidence. Plus, depending on who you believe, the mob may be watching from afar. To sum up, Hil, yes, it is fair to say I have a problem.''

"What are you going to do about it?"

I finished my beer and put the can back in the ice bucket. I shrugged. "Nose around Hinkston's shady operations, maybe. I still need the evidence that Dwight is the thief. Sherm found it. Maybe I can."

"They knew him. He could get into those places. Those people would talk to him."

"But I'm bigger and tougher and smarter."

"And uglier," Hilda said. "Look, if Sherm found what you need, what did he do with it? Did he hide it?"

"Maybe he didn't do anything with it. Maybe he never wrote it down. But that's a good point; maybe he did, too. Want to go over to Patty's tomorrow? Sunday afternoon in the suburbs. You girls can chat about embroidery and cake recipes; I'll toss the house again."

"Sexist lout. Okay, let's." Hilda stretched. It was a long, voluptuous stretch, about a thirteen on a scale of ten. "Now," she said, "would you like to mess around again?"

"Does a bear live in—?"

"Don't start those, especially not the Dan Quayle ones. Be right back." Hilda got off the bed and walked toward the bathroom. I carefully watched her moving away.

"I must be dead," I said, "and, would you believe it, I've gone to heaven."

CHAPTER THIRTY-THREE

The next morning Hilda and I puttered around in her kitchen, doing our usual early Sunday routine. She sliced fruit and heated a coffeecake; I built a blender-load of Ramos gin fizzes. We ate and drank at the kitchen counter with her little television on but turned down. Garrick did his avuncular mortician impression and Mrs. Schwarzenegger crinkled her nose at me, but I couldn't get interested.

I remembered what I'd forgotten to ask Billy Warwick.

"I screwed up again, Hil," I said. "Billy might have taken whatever evidence Sherm had against Dwight. And I didn't even think to ask him."

"Wouldn't Sherm have hidden it?"

"Where? He didn't get it until Wednesday. That's when he'd told Becky Chalmers he was going back 'to ask the right questions.' And he did go back; Mancuso's people tailed him around the Hinkston business circuit that night. Afterward he spent the night in a motel. Assuming he had papers or notes, something like that, not just information he remembered, the stuff could only have been in a few places. The motel, his car, or his pockets."

Hilda looked thoughtful. "He went to work Thursday, didn't he? Would he hide it there?"

"Under Hinkston's nose? Not likely."

"He could have mailed it to himself."

That was possible. It fit in with Sherm's amateur spy tendencies. "Okay, that could be. But his pockets and the car are the most likely places. And if Dwight knew Sherm had something, he could have told Billy to search for it after he hit him."

I phoned the cop shop and asked for Sergeant Ricco. Ricco was off; Ed Durkee was on. Ed wasn't too happy about that. "I hate Sunday duty," he said. "What do you want?"

"Two things." I told him what I was looking for, but I didn't mention Billy Warwick. "Remember the night before Sherm Akister was killed? Mancuso's people tailed him to a Motel 6. Has anyone checked to see if he left anything in the room? Or put it in the safe, maybe? Or even left it to be mailed?"

"Do they have a safe?" Ed said. "I don't know. Good point, though. What else?"

"Sherm's car. Was it searched?"

"I thought of that the other day, after you told me about this Stapner no-good, so I checked. The car was searched—"

"Really searched, not just—"

"Really searched, goddamn it. There was nothing there like you want."

"Damn! Had it been broken into?"

"Legally, maybe, but not the way you mean. It was unlocked."

Way to go, Sherm, you . . .

Ed said, "I'll run down the motel angle. Call me back in an hour or two." He hung up.

"The car was clean," I told Hilda. "We're almost out of places for it to be."

"You don't want to search his house now?"

"No need. He didn't go near there after he had the information."

"I already phoned Patty. She's expecting us."

"I know. We'll go over and see how she's getting along. After that, though, you want to go for a ride, see the sights?"

"What sights?"

"Couple of whorehouses, a hot-car garage, maybe a finance company where they break your leg if you miss a payment."

"Tell you what, big guy," Hilda said. "You really know how to show a girl a good time."

I'd heard Hilda's side of the phone call to Patty; it was strictly "if you're going to be home, we'll drop by; don't make a fuss."

A man would believe that; when you got there, he'd still be watching the ball game. No fuss. You'd be offered cold beer, maybe, or hot coffee. Food might be potato chips for a snack or a frozen pizza for a meal, depending on many things, none of them being your phone call.

Women are more civilized. When Hilda and I arrived at Patty Akister's she welcomed us into a spotless house that smelled like a bakery. There was an apple pie three inches high cooling on a rack in the kitchen. It tasted as good as it smelled. This was maybe an hour after brunch at Hilda's, so I didn't do the pie justice. Barely got through my second helping.

Patty seemed to be in pretty good shape. She was cheerful without being manic, and she had obviously taken pains with her appearance before we came. Those seemed to be good signs to me.

But she was still worried about why Sherm's spy-masters hadn't contacted her. Damn!

"Wouldn't you think they'd at least send me a letter, Mr. Rafferty? I'm disappointed, I really am. I've been thinking about contacting them. I don't know exactly where to start, but—"

"I don't think that's a good idea, Patty," I said.

"But why not?" Patty crossed her chubby arms and looked at me intently. Her bright blue eyes were confused and maybe something else, too. Hurt? Indignant?

Hilda developed a sudden sharp interest in a crumb on her pie plate.

"Everything's under control, Patty," I said. Hilda glanced up sceptically.

"I wish I could believe that," Patty said.

Rafferty's Rule Number Forty-seven: When in trouble, lie like a son of a bitch.

"Well, he asked me not to tell you yet, but . . . Deputy Director Galsworthy called me on Friday."

Patty beamed. "I knew it would happen!"

Hilda rolled her eyes then dredged up a fixed smile when Patty turned, still grinning, toward her.

"Isn't that wonderful?" Patty said.

"Wonderful," Hilda said. "Who'd have guessed?"

"Oh, please, Mr. Rafferty, which agency is it? Because Sherm was never allowed to tell, you see."

"Ah. Well, I shouldn't, either. Let's just call it a very large organization with a three-letter name." I figured that covered everything: CIA, FBI, NBC, FHA. . . .

Patty's eyes went even wider. She bit her lower lip. "I was right, then! I thought it was the—"

"Please! I can't say any more."

Hilda rolled her eyes again.

"You have to understand, Patty," I said, "they're proceeding slowly, but that's normal in the case of, ah, undercover operatives." I found myself wishing I'd read more spy novels. I didn't know the jargon well enough for this.

Patty couldn't sit still. She bounced slightly in her chair as I lied about the situation being monitored by Sherm's deep-cover partners, the need for patience, and the certainty that Sherm's contribution to modern espionage would be recognized and remembered. When I started to run down, Patty helped me con her.

"I guess they contacted you because you're in the same business," she said. "Sherm told me they are very cautious about outsiders, even wives."

"Ah, right," I said. "It's all done on a need-to-know basis." Uh-oh, I thought suddenly, was need-to-know spies? Or was that only the military?

If I was wrong, Patty didn't catch it. "One more thing," I said to her. "I'm way out of line telling you this, so you have to keep it quiet. Deputy Director, ah, Galsworthy is trying to arrange something special. I can't say what. It is very unusual, but for Sherm, well . . . The point is, you shouldn't say anything or try to contact the department. That would ruin Galsworthy's plans."

"Oh, I won't," Patty said. "And thank you so much for telling me."

After that Hilda and I got out as quickly as we could. Patty stood at the curb and waved as we drove away. A block later Hilda said, "I can't stand it. What in the world are you going to do? What if she wants to talk to this Goldsworthy character you made up?"

"Galsworthy," I said. "I'll think of something."

"You'd better, or you'll break her heart."

"Yeah, that's what I'm afraid of, too."

I found a phone booth and called Ed. "Too bad," he said. "The motel angle didn't work out. Good thinking, though."

"Thanks. If I ever want to be a cop again, I'll put you down as a reference."

"Don't bother," Ed said.

I gave Hilda the promised tour of Hinkston's Wonderful World of Crime, but it wasn't particularly impressive. Mostly the names and addresses on the list Mancuso had given me didn't look like much on a sunny Sunday afternoon.

One of the whorehouses was an apartment like the one where Sherm had died. Boring. The other one was a roach-hole in the industrial area just over the river. Two girls, one black, one white, stood on the sidewalk in front of a grubby building with NUDE MODELS painted on the front. The girls wore clothes, sort of, but there wasn't much doubt that minor problem could be easily dealt with.

Several girls came out, looked around, went back in. The place seemed to be suffering through a Sunday afternoon slump. I bet myself Saturday nights weren't like that. After fifteen minutes we left.

Hinkston's hot-car garage was closed. Sunday is not a particularly good day for crimefighters.

The address for the shylocking operation turned out not to be one of those one-location finance companies, after all. It was a tiny grocery store on a street corner in a part of town where the cops only go in pairs with shotguns. I didn't have a shotgun with me, so I took the big military Colt out of the glove compartment and tucked it under my right thigh. Hilda gulped when I did that.

Two groups of teenage boys leaned against the grimy walls of the grocery, one group on each side of the entrance, on different streets. One group was brown; the other was black. A large tattooed white man looked out the grocery-store door as we idled slowly around the corner. Faces of three colors—brown, black, and white—stared at us with hate and distrust. Racial harmony is where you find it.

"Don't you dare stop this car," Hilda said.

"No. Dry run today, that's all."

"Run," she said. "I like the sound of that."

When we were almost back to her house, Hilda said softly, "Do you think you'll be able to find what you need at any of those places?"

"No, not really."

"If you don't, do you know what to do next?"

"No."

CHAPTER THIRTY-FOUR

The garage didn't look like much at first glance. It was a narrow building perhaps twenty years old. It needed a coat of paint. Metal sandwich signs out front said AUTOMOTIVE ELECTRICIAN and MECHANIC ON DUTY and HONK FOR SERVICE.

Inside the workshop was small. An old dark blue Plymouth and a Ford pickup filled it up. One mechanic leaned under the hood of the Plymouth; a pair of coveralled legs protruded from the open door of the pickup. Nearby, at a secondhand desk in the corner, another man talked on a telephone and wrote things down on a yellow pad with greasy fingerprints on it.

A steel-topped workbench was littered with hand tools. There were no fancy electronic diagnostic gadgets here; the closest thing to high tech was a timing light strobing busily under the Plymouth's hood. An elderly radio blasted country-and-western music at a volume that allowed conversation but didn't make it easy.

Just another down-home little garage. A small business scraping along. Grass-roots free enterprise.

Uh-huh.

But I'd driven around the block and down the alley, and I knew the building went back much farther than it looked from the street. The back wall of the workshop—the one with the padlocked door on it—was at least forty feet from the actual back of the building. And the real back wall, on the alley side, had a large roller door. Which was closed. And locked.

There was a large room in there where they disguised the stolen cars or broke them down for parts. Supersleuth strikes again.

I wondered if I would be able to hear machinery through the workshop back wall if I leaned against it. I hadn't even gotten close when the man on the telephone hung up abruptly and called out, "Kin I help you?" He pronounced it "hep." He got up and came toward me.

"Yeah," I said. I had to half shout over the insistent twang of the radio. "Dwight said I should see you about getting rid of—"

He shook his head and grinned apologetically. "Cain't hear for shit in here. C'mon out front." He motioned me ahead of him. We went outside. It was smoothly done.

" 'At's better," he said. "It ain't worth the trouble turning the radio down. Five minutes those boys got it up again even louder. And they ain't done a lick of work in the meantime." He was a short, barrel-like man in his early forties, with thinning hair and a button nose. He shoved his hands into his hip pockets and squinted up at me. "Now what can I do fer you?"

"Dwight said you might be able to handle some cars for me."

He smiled vaguely. "Dwight? I'm sorry, partner, I don't . . ." He shrugged at me.

"I can get whatever you want.'Vettes, Cads, Mercedes, whatever."

"Hell, we'll fix anything," he said. "Anything we can, at least. But I don't think that's what you're talking about, is it?"

"No. Look, you want a nice '90 Corvette? Red, with only two thousand miles on it. I can have it here in an hour, but I gotta have a decent price for it." I wasn't sure what a hot Corvette was worth; I should have found out. Preparation is everything.

"Man, I wish I could afford me one of them. Marge'd love it. But, look, partner, we don't sell cars. Or buy 'em, either. We only fix 'em. You understand now?" He smiled up at me hopefully, as if he was explaining street directions to a befuddled foreign tourist.

"That's not what Dwight Stapner said."

The man shrugged again. "I wouldn't know, partner."

"Well, hell," I said. "Hey, has Sherm been around lately? I haven't seen him for a week or so."

He shook his head. "Don't know him."

"I guess I made a mistake," I said.

"No problem. Hey, you ever need any work done on that Mustang, you come see us, you hear?"

He was still standing out front with his hands in his hip pockets when I drove away. Just a country boy trying to be nice, helping out a confused stranger.

My ass.

I stopped at a police supply store and bought a set of hand-cuffs to replace the pair that went away with Billy Warwick. I don't care what they say about inflation being down; have you noticed the price of handcuffs lately?

* * *

Ten-twenty A.M. My office. Becky Chalmers had phoned. The service said she wouldn't leave a number; she was phoning every half-hour until she reached me. The woman at the service sounded relieved that I was now available to answer my own phone.

I made coffee, waved at Beth Woodland through the big plate-glass window between our offices, and waited.

The mail came. Three bills; one check. Story of my life.

At ten thirty-five Becky called again.

"You've got to help me, Rafferty. Please. Look, I mean this, whatever it takes, whatever you want from me, it's yours. Sex, money, what—"

"Good old Burridge about to dump you, is he?"

"He says today's the last day. He says I owe him two hundred a day since Tues—"

"*You* owe him? What about Lois?"

"She's gone. Burr's taking her to catch a flight to Chicago right now. That's where she's from, Chicago. She paid him, and he took her to the airport. But I don't have anywhere to go. I'm scared."

"Go to the cops, Becky. It's time now."

She drew a ragged breath. Long pause. "Okay. Just don't let him . . . I'm not used to this. I've never worked streets or had people want to . . ." She seemed to get a grip on herself. "All right. I'll tell them whatever they want, as long as I get protection. How do we do that?"

"Sit tight for now. I'll set it up. Where are you?"

"Oh, Christ, Burr would kill me if I told you. Can I call you back? When?"

I said, "When will Burridge be back? He's part of this, too."

"Around one, I think. Is that all right?"

"It's fine, Becky. Call me when he's there. I'll lay the groundwork now; we'll firm it up then."

"Oh, God, that sounds good."

"It'll all work out. You might not like parts of it, but it will work out. Relax."

"Thank you. And, seriously, I mean it. Whatever you want, I'll—"

"Call me when Burridge gets back."

"Bye." Wistful, almost little-girlish. I wondered which of the Beckys I'd seen and heard so far was the real one.

"Mancuso," I said, "you want a witness against Manny Hinkston?"

The phone was silent for what seemed an hour or two, then Mancuso said, "Sure. What's up?"

I told him about Becky. "Tell you the truth, I don't know how much her testimony does for you." Whoops, I'd forgotten he didn't know Warwick was dead. "Of course, she saw the guy who killed Sherm. That's something. And she ran a whorehouse for Hinkston."

"I want to talk to her," he said. "Bring her in."

"Well, it's not quite that easy." I went through the situation quickly. Talking to Mancuso on the phone, I found myself speaking rapidly and compressing everything; saving time when I spoke because he was so slow when it was his turn.

"Her pimp will want to meet somewhere," Mancuso said. "That's okay. I'll do that."

"They don't know you. I'd better come, too."

"Okay. Let me know where and when. If I'm not here, Bromley can find me."

I'd hung up and poured myself a cup of coffee before I realized I might have cut Mancuso off before he could say good-bye.

"I think this is best, Rafferty," Hilda said.

"Might be hard on Patty, though. News coverage, a trial; Sherm's part in it is bound to come out."

By three o'clock everything had been set up. Mancuso and I would meet Burridge and Beck at nine-thirty that night in a restaurant parking lot on North Central Expressway. I'd already checked out the location; it wasn't ideal, but it would do.

But that was for later; early dinner with Hilda was for now. We were trying a new German place. Hilda had ordered schnitzel and salad; I had a giant rare T-bone, potato skins with double sour cream, onion rings, and a cold bottle of Tuborg. What's the German work for cholesterol?

"You're underestimating Patty," Hilda said. "She's more resilient than you think."

"Maybe. She's fixated on that hero-secret-agent idea, though. Finding out Sherm was a bagman will be a helluva shock to her."

Hilda sliced her schnitzel. "You don't have a choice. Saving Patty embarrassment can't justify letting that woman Becky be killed, even if she is only a whore."

"Whores are people, too, Hil."

"I know. I shouldn't have said that. But . . ."

She put down her knife and fork. "Rafferty, don't you know that most women feel threatened by prostitutes?"

"Nope. Why?"

"Maybe threatened isn't the right word, but . . . Anyone who has sex with hundreds of strangers is, well, scary. There's the disease thing, of course, especially now. But there's also something else, something competitive, I guess. We don't like to admit it—again especially now—but women compete for men's attention."

"Here's a hot flash from the newsroom. Men compete for women's attention. Film at ten."

"No, I mean women like to feel they're sexy. Maybe sexier than other women. And who's more openly sexual than a prostitute? Even though being a prostitute would be repugnant."

"Love you, babe, but that's silly."

Hilda smiled. "I know. I just listened to myself. I didn't express it quite right, perhaps, but there's something there, believe me."

"I think you're confusing being sexual and being sexy."

"Perhaps."

"I'm available for consultations on such matters. Would you like an appointment later this evening?"

"I'll let you know," she said, and winked.

"Now that's sexy."

"Oh, good," Hilda said.

CHAPTER THIRTY-FIVE

Mancuso—leather bomber jacket, Hush Puppies, and all—stood on the curb near the underground parking-garage entrance of the downtown cop shop. I stopped, he got in, I pulled away. "Let's do it," I said.

Mancuso nodded. He nodded faster than he talked.

"Go for it," I said. "That strong silent image works for you."

He nodded again. Mancuso was on a roll; he'd cut his communication time in half.

Headed out on North Central Expressway, I said, "Are you going to arrest her or go for protective custody?"

A hundred yards later, he said, "Protective custody. At first, anyway. If she plays fair, that'll give her a safe place to sleep. If she goes forgetful on me, I'll bust her for conspiracy."

"She's scared," I said. "She's ready to talk."

"No problem then."

Burridge had picked a steakhouse parking lot for the meet. It was eleven past nine when I tucked the Mustang into the back row facing out. There were no other cars in that row, only six or eight in the next row, and a dozen or more up close to the restaurant building. Mancuso and I got out, walked through the lot, checked each parked car, then went back to sit in the Mustang.

At nine-thirty Burridge's silver Cadillac pulled into the lot and flicked its lights. Mancuso and I got out and leaned against the Mustang. The Cad turned toward us, went between the first and second rows, then looped back so it was pointed toward the entrance as it oozed nearer to us. There were two men in the front seat. Burridge was one, and that was probably his bodyguard Donald behind the wheel. Donald had a lot to learn about guarding bodies. For one thing, you keep your hands free.

The back door of the Cad opened before the car had completely stopped. Becky Chalmers jumped out as soon as she could.

"Hi," she said. "Is this the cop who's—"

She was two steps from the Cad, about the same from me, when the bullet took her high in the chest. She went down with a startled look on her face and her arms out wide. A large soft bag she carried hit the ground; a shoe fell out.

I was down by then, too, flat on the asphalt, trying to work out where the shooter was and yelling "Down, goddamn it. Down!" at Mancuso.

The crack of the rifle was still reverberating when the wheels of the silver Cad whirled blue tire smoke at me. The big car howled away.

"Shit!" I heard Mancuso say, two beats behind the action as usual.

The second shot was a miss. It chewed a trench in the parking lot fifteen feet away, and then I had the shooter pegged. He was on Mancuso's side of the Mustang, toward the rear. But where? He couldn't be shooting from the expressway; that was too low along here. The parallel access road?

I had strapped on the .38 for the meet, but it wasn't much firepower against a big-bore rifle. Still . . .

I popped up for a look then came back down instantly to interpret what I'd seen. It's funny how you remember old tricks like that when you need them.

Mancuso had gotten his butt away from the fender, but he was still fumble-footing his way around the car to my side. How could he be so slow?

Beyond him, maybe thirty yards from us, a van had stopped on the access road. The sliding door on the side was open.

As I popped back up that open door blazed with a muzzle flash. I barely heard a grunt and the scuff of leather behind the rifle's crack. I forced myself up from my automatic flinch and put three slugs where the muzzle flash had been. I tried to, anyway. At thirty yards with a two-inch barrel, all you can do is try.

Mancuso was down, sprawled in the open area in front of the Mustang. His left arm had developed another elbow; the leather jacket was dark there. Not far from him Becky Chalmers lay with her cheek crushed against the rough asphalt. Her eyes were wide and empty.

I scuttled out, grabbed Mancuso's closest ankle, and dragged him behind the Mustang. His broken arm flopped and bounced. He screamed.

There was another shot, duller and not as loud that time. Different gun. Maybe I got the first shooter after all. Then a motor revved high and dopplered away. When I sneaked a look, the van was gone.

Mancuso swore. "Hurts," he said. "Jesus, that hurts."

I stood up and slumped against the Mustang. My hand was shaking so much I almost dropped the .38, so I put the gun away. It only took two tries.

People came cautiously out of the steakhouse; the first sirens began a long way away. A thin blond waitress ran up with her arms full of tablecloths. She said, "I thought . . . bandages?"

I ripped a long strip off one tablecloth and put a tourniquet on Mancuso's arm. She rolled up another one to put behind his head.

I spread the third tablecloth over Becky Chalmers. It didn't seem quite right, the way people stood there and stared at her.

CHAPTER THIRTY-SIX

"Goddamn, Rafferty!" Ed Durkee said. "This is a major screwup, even for you."

"Bullshit," I said.

It was almost three o'clock in the morning now. We'd been sitting in Ed's office for two hours. Before that we'd waltzed around an interrogation room for a while. Before that they'd questioned me at the scene. Before that we'd sent Mancuso off in a yelping ambulance and before *that* . . . well, you know about before that.

"Bullshit," I said again. "For one thing, I didn't shoot him, and for another, he's awful easy to shoot. You never saw anybody move so slow."

The word from the hospital was good, considering. The slug had shattered Mancuso's upper arm. The humerus, they called that bone. Some name. There was damage, a lot of it, but the bone docs were already sticking the bone back together with pins and screws and . . . who knows? Superglue, maybe.

The big artery in his upper arm had been nicked, too, but that was fixed now. Mancuso owed the waitress with the tablecloths a big one.

Mancuso would be all right eventually, but that didn't calm down the cops. The whole force was steamed. They were angry and frustrated and a little worried, too, because Mancuso's wound reminded them of their own mortality. It's scary when your friends go down.

At least, that's the way I felt when I was a cop and the "officer down" calls went out.

All that tension had to dissipate somewhere. I was handy. So far tonight I'd been peered at—and sometimes yelled at— by a deputy chief, a captain, two lieutenants, and I'd quit counting the sergeants a couple of hours ago.

It was down to just Ed Durkee and Ricco now, and they'd gotten most of it out of their systems.

"Hell, Ed, Rafferty's got a point," Ricco said. "Goddamn Mancuso is one slow son of a bitch."

Ed rubbed his malleable hound-dog face. "Don't let the IU guys hear you say that. They want me to charge Rafferty."

"With what?" I said.

Ed shrugged. "They don't much care. Tell me about it one more time." No cop will believe anything until he's heard it twelve times.

I described the shooting yet again.

"A big rifle, huh?" Ricco said. "Not an automatic weapon?"

"The rate of fire was too slow." We'd been through this before.

"An AK on single fire?"

"No. AKs chug. This gun cracked. My guess is a bolt-action deer rifle. That would be about the right fire rate and sound."

Ed grunted. "Could be. The slug from Mancuso's arm was too messed up to be sure, but it weighs out right for a 30.06." That was new.

"That fits," I said. "An old sporterized Springfield; something like that."

Ed nodded; Ricco hiked his thin shoulders beneath his gaudy sports jacket; we all sat there like lumps for a while. Finally I said, "Are you going to pick up Dwight Stapner?"

Ed groaned. This was not the first time tonight I'd brought up the subject of Dwight Stapner.

"For God's sake, Rafferty, will you give it a rest? How

many times do I have to tell you? Stapner was across town
in a restaurant when the shooting went down. He's got twenty
people to say so."

"So he didn't pull the trigger. So what? Dwight hired it
done. Maybe his people tailed Burridge; maybe Burridge
sold out. Either way, this is down to Dwight Stapner. Who
else would want to waste Becky Chalmers?"

"You say. Because that's what Chalmers told you. Hell,
it was only hearsay when she was alive. Now . . . ?" Ed
shrugged.

Ricco cut in. "Face it, Rafferty. We ain't got shit on Stapner."

"Get something, then. Dwight did it."

"Probably so. I hope we can prove that some day." Ed
rubbed his face again. "Let's get out of here. I think I remember what sleep is like. I want to go see if I'm right."

Ed gave me a lift back to the steakhouse parking lot. The
excitement had long since passed. The prowl cars and am-
bulances and medical examiners and detective teams were
gone. So were the restaurant staff and diners. The lot was
empty, except for my Mustang. Cowboy sat on its hood.

Ed stopped twenty yards away and said, "Aw, Christ, get
out now. I'm gonna pretend I don't see your gunslinger pal
over there."

I did; Ed left. When I walked up to the Mustang, Cowboy
slid off the hood and stretched. "Took you long enough."

"What's up?"

"You need lookin' after, Rafferty. That sucker Dwight's
on the prod now."

"He's alibied for tonight. The cops can't touch him."

Cowboy snorted. "*Won't* touch him, more likely. How
'bout you? You ready to take him out yet?"

"Cowboy, we can't just go out and blast him."

"Mebbe you can't," Cowboy said, "but I sure as hell
can."

CHAPTER THIRTY-SEVEN

I got up at seven A.M. to call Hilda.

"I thought you were coming over last night late," she said. "I thought up all these wonderful examples of sexy, and I wanted your advice."

I told her about Becky and Mancuso.

"Oh, my God. Are you all right?"

"I'm fine, babe. He wasn't after me. And Mancuso only got shot because he stood around in the way."

"I hate this," she said.

"It's over now, probably. Dwight Stapner has cleaned up his last loose end. He's home free."

"How do you feel about that?"

"Shitty," I said.

"You're sure you're all right?"

"Yeah. Cowboy's here, anyway. Anyone after me—and no one is—would have to try it with tactical nukes."

"Well, be careful. . . ."

After we hung up, I went back to bed. A shooting, five hours of police questions, and only two hours sleep left me feeling tired. I must be getting old.

When Cowboy kicked the bed it dragged me up out of a dark, foreboding sleep. The smell of cooking breakfast fought with the old-sweat-sock taste in my mouth.

"Eleven o'clock, boss-man. Up and at 'em. Bacon and eggs in five."

"Ymmph."

Ten minutes later Cowboy slid scrambled eggs onto two plates and handed me one. We sat down to eat. Cowboy wore his hat at the table. He'd worn his hat while he cooked, too. I tried to think of the times when I'd seen Cowboy without his hat. There weren't many.

He chewed solemnly, swallowed, and said, "That Becky gal thought she was gonna be safe with you, but they got her. I 'spect you want ole Dwight pretty bad now."

"I want him," I said. "So do you."

Cowboy nodded. "That's a fact. You think on what I said last night?"

"About blasting him? That's not my style, Cowboy. I can't just—"

"What he's doing to everybody else, ain't it?"

"True."

"From what you say, the cops ain't gonna do nothing 'bout him. Somebody ought to."

I sipped coffee to buy time. Finally I said, "I'd rather see if I can help the cops put him away."

Cowboy sniffed. "Ain't gonna work, but we'll play it your way. Mebbe we'll git lucky. Not the way you think, I mean mebbe we'll spook him into trying something personal-like. I s'pose it'd be all right to waste him then."

"If Dwight shoots at us, we shoot back."

"Jest wanted to git it clear in my mind," Cowboy said. He shook his head. "I do worry 'bout you from time to time, Rafferty. You keep gitting foolish ideas 'bout playing fair."

I called Ed Durkee a little before one o'clock. "What's new?"

He grunted. "Not much. They just phoned through the prelim on the Chalmers post-mortem. That slug wasn't banged up as bad as the one Mancuso caught. They say it looks like a 30.06. So you were right about the deer-rifle angle. You want to try for a name to go with that?"

"Don't we wish," I said. "Uh, what about Dwight?"

"You don't quit, do you? Point me toward somebody who will say Dwight hired them to pull the trigger. Do that and I'll bust Stapner."

"Try Roosevelt Burridge, fashion plate and pimp. Burridge might have told Dwight about the meet. You get Burridge to admit that, and you've got Dwight nailed. It's circumstantial evidence, but it's pretty good."

"Yeah, it's good, and so was the last Saturday Night Movie." Ed sighed a long, rumbling whoosh of frustration. "Ricco is sweating your pimp pal right now."

"What does Burridge say?"

"He says Dwight who, and I just gave her a lift, and where's my lawyer; that's what he says. We're gonna have to turn him loose any minute."

"Goddamn," I said.

"Yeah, I know how you feel."

Cowboy and I went to see Mancuso. I went up to the room; Cowboy waited in the hospital lobby.

Mancuso didn't look as bad as he probably felt. He was pale, and his arm was all bandaged up, and he had tubes leading in and out of him, but he was awake and mentally sharp.

He still talked in slow motion, though. You'd think while they had him opened up, they'd have turned up his thermostat.

"Thanks," he said. "I felt naked laying out there in the open. I was sure he was going to shoot again."

"No sweat." We fumbled through the usual hospital food cliches, then I said, "Anything new on Manny Hinkston?"

Mancuso looked at me oddly. Maybe Hilda was right; maybe I didn't do casual as well as I thought.

"What do you mean?" Mancuso said eventually.

"You Intelligence Unit guys are up-to-date on everything that moves. Without Becky Chalmers, can you bust Hinkston? Or Dwight Stapner?"

Mancuso wriggled in his bed and grimaced. "Arm hurts some," he said. "No, without her, it doesn't look too good. That Hinkston outfit is getting weirder by the day, but we don't have anything decent to take to the DA. It's like this."

He nodded at his wounded arm. "You and I both know who did it, but how can I prove it?"

Then a nurse came and ran me out before I "overtired the officer." When I left, an assistant chief in full uniform came up the corridor toward Mancuso's room. He looked too grim to be on a morale-building mission. On the other hand, if I had all those buttons and doohickeys to keep polished, I'd look grim, too.

Downstairs Cowboy uncoiled himself from an uncomfortable-looking green chair and fell into step with me. "Your cop friend okay?"

"Yeah. He looks better than he did last night."

"Chief or something went through here a few minutes ago. My, didn't he look purty, too."

"I saw him." We went through the big doors and out into the sunshine. "Mancuso says they aren't even close to getting Hinkston and Stapner."

Cowboy resettled his hat a half-inch lower on his seamed forehead. "I ain't gonna say it," he rumbled, "but . . ."

"You told me so."

"Well, now that you mention it."

Back at my house, I phoned Hilda at work. Ramon went to find her, reluctantly, being even more snotty than he usually was. Cowboy came back from the kitchen with two beers, handed me one, then turned on the television with the volume very low. He squatted in front of it and chuckled.

"Oh, hi, sweetheart." Hilda sounded winded when she came to the phone. She'd been outside, she told me, about to leave for an appointment. "What can I do for you?"

"I won't keep you, babe. I'm having a little case of the megrims here. The bad guys are getting away with it this time, and I don't know what to do."

"Maybe this is one of those times when you can't do anything."

"That's a tough concept for a guy like me to grasp."

"It's called real life."

"I'm not ready for tricky stuff like that," I said. "Anybody over there need beating up? Ramon springs to mind."

"That might not be so easy, dear. Ramon does that tae kwan do thing, you know."

"I'll bring a tire iron."

"Sorry," Hilda said. "I need him the way he is."

"Damn. You want to go out for dinner tonight?"

"I have that association dinner meeting. I thought I told you."

"You probably did, babe. No problem."

We said good-bye, and I hung up. Cowboy still squatted in front of the television, chuckling softly, his hat shoved onto the back of his head.

"Glad to see someone having a good time," I said.

"Damndest thing," he said. "Don't know how they get folks to say such silly stuff."

"What are you watching? A soap opera?"

He snapped off the television and stood up, grinning widely. "Donahue."

I renailed a loose step at the back door then prowled through the house looking for another chore where I could hit something, anything. I couldn't find one, so I got another beer and sprawled on the couch to drink it. Then I fell asleep and woke up hours later when the phone rang. As I stumbled toward the phone, I looked at my watch. Six forty-eight. Some nap.

"Haho," I said, coughed, and tried again. "Hello."

It was Patty Akister. Her voice was strained.

"I'm sorry to trouble you with this, Mr. Rafferty, but I've thought about it and I—"

"What's the problem, Patty?" Maybe something was wrong with my diet. How could anyone's mouth taste like this?

"Well, it's about Mr. Stapner, from Sherm's work." Her voice trembled a little at the end.

Now I was wide awake. "Did he hurt you, Patty?"

"No, not really. He only grabbed my arm once."

"Is he gone?"

Cowboy stepped into the room with a quizzical look on his face and his finger in a copy of *Western Horseman*.

"Oh, yes," Patty said, "that was early this afternoon. I just didn't know whether or not to . . ."

"You did the right thing. Tell me what happened."

She did. Dwight had appeared with his blond goon at the door. He wanted in, and he wouldn't take no for an answer. He pestered her about those "sales records" again, which meant that Billy Warwick had not found Sherm's evidence of Dwight's thievery after all.

Patty said Dwight kept her in her kitchen—he'd only blocked her way, she said, he didn't grab her, except that one time—while his thug ransacked Sherm's spare bedroom-study. As far as Patty knew, he hadn't found anything.

"But it's a terrible mess, Mr. Rafferty. And it's not right, is it? They're not allowed to do that? Are they?"

"No, they're not. I'll take care of it. Why don't you call Mrs. Holmiston? See if she can come over."

"She's here now," Patty said. "Oh, wait just a—"

Wilma Holmiston, tough as old boots, came onto the phone with a gruff, "Rafferty?"

"How is she?"

"She's all right. For now. But you better get this sorted out, young man." She said a great deal even though she couldn't say much, not with Patty beside her.

"Stay with her, Mrs. Holmiston. I'll handle it."

"You do that." She hung up. The old gal would have made a helluva top sergeant.

I went to the kitchen, drank a glass of water, then tapped out the number for Manny Hinkston's furniture store. They'd be closed; it was almost seven o'clock. I hoped it wasn't too late.

It wasn't. A gravelly voice answered and admitted Manny was there. He came to the phone with a snarled, "The fuck you want now, Rafferty?"

"I want to talk to you about Dwight, Hinkston. You've got problems you don't know about."

"*I've* got problems? Your *ass*! You're the one—"

"Stapner leaned on Sherm Akister's wife today. What happened to our deal?"

"What happened? What happened? I'll tell you what happened, you two-bit dog turd! Dwight found out you was covering for that fucking Sherm. That bitch had the money all the time. Dwight got it today."

I felt a little sick. Everytime I turned around Dwight pulled another one out of the hat. "He's shining you on," I said. "He's been skimming from all your operations. All he did today was throw a couple of bucks back to dump the blame onto Sherm."

"What kinda dumbass you think I am? And where do you get off—" He was raving now; his voice had gone high and breathy, like he was hyperventilating.

"I'm not going to argue with you, Manny. Lay off Patty Akister. Don't let Dwight lean on her again."

"Lay off her?" Hinkston screamed. "You . . . you lay off *me*, you fucking . . ." He was out of control; his voice was distorted, hard to understand. "I'll lean on anybody I fucking want, you asshole. Sherm's bitch or you or . . . Aw, I'm sick of ya!" The phone went dead.

I hung up. Cowboy looked at me.

"You were right," I said. "Dwight and Hinkston both. Let's take them out now, before somebody else gets hurt."

Cowbody nodded. "I knowed you'd see the light, sooner or later."

CHAPTER THIRTY-EIGHT

"We have to do it," I said to Cowboy, "but I don't like it."

Cowboy shrugged as he thumbed fat .44-magnum cartridges into a speedloader. "Mimi's gotta cousin who pumps out septic tanks. He don't like that much, either. It's just something that's got to be done."

I turned off Garland Road a block short of Hinkston's store, then into an alley that ran behind the building. I stopped the Mustang as soon as we were in shadow. We got out. At the other end of the alley, on the left, the back of Hinkston's building was a black mass in the dimness. Half a block away traffic hummed along Garland Road. Something scuttled along the alley and a cat yowled somewhere.

I opened the Mustang's trunk; we lifted out the shotguns, checked the magazines, and dumped extra shells into our pockets. Cowboy's shotgun was a newish Ithaca 37, the police model with a pistol grip instead of a shoulder stock. I had an Ithaca, too. Mine was twenty years older and had seen several duck seasons before I started pointing it at people.

Cowboy slapped his pockets and loosened the big Ruger in his shoulder holster; I shoved the .45 into my belt in back and closed the Mustang's trunk.

"Let's go," I said.

Cowboy worked the slide of his shotgun; I did the same. The metallic *snicks* echoed softly in the dark alley. There is no sound more purposeful than the tight rattle of a pump shotgun being readied for work.

There were three doors in the back wall of Hinkston's building; two industrial roller doors, like garage doors but much larger, and a normal-size door nearby. The smaller door was metal, too. It was locked.

Cowboy said, "You s'posed to be good at this, boss-man. Do your stuff."

I dug out my lockpins and worked on the lock for a time. I'm not very good a picking locks; I can usually fumble my way past the sort of junk most houses have on their back doors, but this was a healthy commercial item. "We may have to wait for them to come out, Cowboy. I'm not sure I can get this thing open."

"Well, for . . ." He wandered aimlessly back and forth in the alley. On the third pass he went over to the roller doors and tried one then the other.

The second door was unlocked; it rolled upward a foot and a half. It was noisy but not as loud as I'd have thought it would be.

"Damn!" Cowboy said, holding his shotgun aimed at the wide, low opening. "Ain't that something?"

I put my lockpicks away. "I must have unlocked the wrong one by mistake."

"Haw, haw," Cowboy said softly. "You want to make any more noise, or you want to go underneath?"

"Underneath," I said. "But let me have a good look inside first."

Cowboy dropped to one knee, shotgun ready, while I sprawled outside the roller door and gingerly peered underneath.

It was very dark in their. Hadn't Hinkston ever heard of leaving lights on inside to discourage burglars? There was a wide archway about thirty feet away outlined by a dim glow beyond it. This area in back would be where they shipped furniture in and out, I decided. Through the arch was the showroom. And that faint glow came from the lights in the office loft above the showroom.

After a few minutes my eyes adjusted; I began to make out shapes in the gloom. There was a car in there. Hinkston's, probably. There were bulky, square-cornered shapes, too. Those would be boxes of chairs and sofas and beds. Most importantly there was no movement and no sound.

I turned sideways, rolled under the door, and came up with my shotgun pointed out into the blackened room. Deadeye Rafferty, ready to waste the boogey-men. "Okay," I hissed.

There was a soft scuffle as Cowboy came under the door. I felt him stand up beside me. We automatically stepped into a defensive pattern, facing out from the door, but half turned to cover each other's back. It felt good, and I marveled again at how the old skills and habit patterns came back at the right time.

From here on our task was straightforward. We'd cover and move, cover and move, as we'd done so many other times. Into the showroom first. Then a reconnoiter. Should we go up the stairs after Dwight and Hinkston, sucker them downstairs, or simply wait for them to come down at their own speed?

Whichever we decided, it would be dirty work. Cowboy had it pegged, though. It was a job that had to be done.

While I stood there, feeling lean and mean and sneaky as

hell, an electric motor started and the big roller door beside my shoulder rumbled closed. Overhead lights came on, and the shipping area exploded into brightness.

"Uh-oh," Cowboy said.

CHAPTER THIRTY-NINE

The lights were so bright, it was hard to see. I felt the pain in my eyes and a sinking feeling in my gut, but mostly I felt stupid. And I felt very close to losing any chance to ever be stupid again.

"Two over here with automatic weapons," Cowboy said behind my shoulder. "How you doing?"

There were three of them on my side; two in blue coveralls and a tall, dapper man in a perfectly tailored dark suit. The gunmen had M-16s and hard eyes and deadpan expressions. They held their M-16s with the butts socketed tightly into their shoulders and their right elbows high. They leaned forward slightly, ready for the recoil. I wondered if their fire selectors were on AUTO and decided they probably were.

The man in the expensive suit had his fingers on the switches which had lowered the door and turned on the lights. He let go now and wiped his hands carefully on a large white handkerchief. He was thirty-five perhaps, with dark hair and a smooth face that wrinkled in distaste at whatever he found on his fingers. I steadied the Ithaca's foresight on his stomach.

"Three here," I said to Cowboy. "Two armed and one who looks like the heavy."

The car I'd barely seen in the gloom was to my half-left now. It wasn't Hinkston's car after all. It was Burridge's silver Cadillac, parked facing away from us. The trunk lid was down but ajar. What the hell?

"Okay?" a strained voice called from beyond the showroom archway.

The dapper man with the handkerchief looked up, annoyed. He opened his mouth to speak, but before he could another voice growled, "Yeah, come on, let's go."

The new voice was older, rougher, deeper. It came from Burridge's Cadillac. Then the driver's door crunched open, and a man got out. He slammed the door, nodded at the sound, and strolled toward us. As he ambled the length of the Cad, he trailed one finger along the fender line and nodded to himself, smiling, like he's just decided to buy the car.

Dapper said, "Mr. Ducello, is it a good idea for you to—?"

I can tell a bigger boss when I see one. I snapped the Ithaca muzzle from Dapper to Ducello. One of the M-16 toters on my side shifted sideways one step then steadied his aim on me again. "Head," he said calmly. The other man said "Chest."

"Mr. Ducello," Dapper said, "this is getting out of hand. He might shoot you."

"Might, hell," I said. "Any loud noises, I'll cut him in half."

Ducello looked at me again. He smiled a tight little smile and waved both hands at the coveralled gunmen. "What do you think they're going to do to you?"

I snugged my cheek tighter against the stock of the Ithaca. "Whatever they do, you won't be here to see it," I said.

Ducello was a squat man in his late fifties. He wore an expensive suit like Dapper's, but it didn't fit him nearly as well. He had black hair going gray and bushy eyebrows. His cheeks were pocked with old acne scars.

The voice in the showroom called out again, "So is it okay or not?"

Ducello yelled over his shoulder, "I already told you, come on."

Two more men shuffled into the room. Each man carried one end of an ungainly green bundle that crinkled as they clumsily lugged it into the shipping area. On the second snap glance I recognized it. It was a body, a big man's body, with very large green plastic bags pulled over the head and feet then taped together around the waist.

The men carrying the body wore khaki work pants and plaid shirts. They shuffled awkwardly toward the trunk of the Cad.

"Don't let them get between us," I said to Ducello. The Ithaca was becoming heavy. The grip was slippery with sweat. My face was wet with sweat, too, and my eyes stung from the salt of it.

Ducello slowly sidestepped away from the Cad. He made no effort to duck or dodge; he made it easy for me to adjust my aim. "You heard him," he said to the body-haulers. "Watch where you walk." Ducello seemed slightly amused.

"Stapner?" I said to Ducello.

He nodded with a sour look on his face. "Yeah."

The man holding Dwight Stapner's plastic-bagged feet tried to hold them with one hand while he flipped up the Cad's trunk lid with the other. That didn't work, so he and his partner lowered the body until the buttocks were on the concrete floor. Then he got the trunk open, picked up the feet again and the two of them hoisted the corpse.

"One," the man on the shoulders said. "Two. Three!" They grunted and tried to swing-toss Dwight's bulk into the Cad's trunk.

Almost. Dwight's butt caught on the lip of the trunk. "Aw, shit," the foot man said, and they wrestled with the ungainly package until it was in properly.

Once, while they crammed Dwight into the trunk, one of the men tugged at something else in there. He lifted it, and I saw he held a pale suite-coat sleeve. A black hand flopped loosely at the end of the sleeve. He tucked the arm away.

"And I guess that's Burridge," I said.

"Who?" Ducello said. "The nigger pimp?"

The men who'd loaded Dwight blew out their breath, wiped their foreheads, and trudged away, back to the archway and the showroom and offices beyond. They glanced at Cowboy and me once, but, except for the careful way they stayed out of the line of fire, they might not have noticed anything out of the ordinary.

"So what do you want here?" Ducello said to me. "You come for these guys, too?"

"Not Burridge," I said. "But Stapner, yes. And Hinkston."

Ducello nodded. "The boys'll bring Manny down next. You see the problem, Paolo?" He talked to the dapper man with the handkerchief now. "You see how bad things had got in this town? Strangers come around to clean up our shit. Hinkston and this jerkoff Stapner, they got things so screwed up, and nobody noticed? It embarrasses me to think we let things go this far."

"Don't worry on our account," I said. The Ithaca felt like it weighed a hundred pounds. I kept it trained on Ducello's stomach anyway.

Dapper Paolo said, "It's almost time, Mr. Ducello. What are we going to do?"

"Do, Paolo? What's such a problem? You think these guys are gonna shoot me because they don't like the way I talk?"

"Mr. Ducello, I'm afraid I don't understand—"

Ducello jerked his right hand up suddenly; he almost died because he'd forgotten me for that instant. He glanced at me, gave a little shrug, then he spoke low and fast to Paolo. "You don't understand, Paolo. *That's* the problem. People don't understand about things today. They don't know how to do business, how to act. Either that or they're crazy, like Manny. That's why we have problems like this. That's why we get shamed by these . . . these screwballs!" He threw a bitter look at the Cad's trunk.

The two body-haulers came back with Hinkston. Same plastic-bag routine, same shuffle, but they were faster this time. The learning curve, I guess, and then, too, Manny was a little guy compared to Dwight.

Ducello watched them stuff Hinkston's body into the trunk of the Cad. They had to work at it. That was a big trunk, but even so . . . When they'd finished, they stepped back. Ducello walked to the car, taking his time again; watching me track him. "Look at this guy, Paolo. He understands about things. You can tell he knows how to act. Hey," he said to me, "you afraid?"

"Terrified," I said truthfully.

"So what're you gonna do about it?" Ducello said.

"I'm gonna blow your ass away if anybody says boo."

Ducello waved his arms at Paolo again. "You see? These guys know. A man's afraid to die, he's afraid to live. When are you gonna learn? You new guys think you know everything. You and scum like this." Ducello spat into the body-filled trunk, slammed it shut. "They had no honor, these men."

Paolo had heard it all before. He checked his fingernails and shrugged his shoulders to settle his zippy suit. "Yes, Mr. Ducello," he said, but he didn't mean it.

Ducello gave the ceiling a "what can you do?" look, then he said to me, "I'm ready to go. You ready to go?"

"We're ready."

It took a little jiggling and sidestepping, and when Paolo stumbled once we all nearly got killed, but five minutes later we'd shifted into new positions. The roller door was open and the two body-haulers had backed Burridge's Cadillac out. They drove away.

"Get my car," Ducello said to Paolo.

"But, Mr. Ducello . . ."

"Get the goddamn car, Paolo." Ducello's voice sounded like a cell door slamming shut.

Paolo didn't like it, but he went. So did one of the gunmen.

Soon a long black Lincoln ghosted to a stop by the open door. An old green Blazer came up behind. Paolo started to get out from behind the wheel of the Lincoln.

"Don't," I said. He didn't. The guy in the Blazer grinned. He stayed behind the wheel without being told.

"How do you want to do this part?" I said to Ducello.

He shrugged. "Don't matter much. You and me, we could handle it easy, but . . . Tell you what. They—" he waved at the remaining three gunmen "—they get into their truck, I'll stand by my car, and you cover me from over there, just inside the door. Then your buddy hits the switch to close the door. You're in here; we're out there. It's over."

"Okay."

We did all that. As soon as the door dropped below shoulder level, I jumped sideways, behind the brick wall. The door didn't look all that thick to me.

No one cheated, though. Three minutes later, when we opened the small door from the inside and stepped out into the alley, they were gone.

Cowboy and I trudged down the alley toward the Mustang. We stretched and worked our arms, easing out the muscle kinks. Aiming a shotgun at one point for twenty minutes is pure hell on the shoulders and neck.

"Well, that was interesting," I said.

"Yeah," Cowboy said. "Kinda makes you forgit all about sex for a little while, don't it?"

CHAPTER FORTY

"The mob did that?" Hilda said. "They killed their own men? That's incredible."

I had picked Hilda up at her store ten minutes ago. We were going to Patty Akister's house.

"No, it makes sense. When you rake in money like the mob does, you don't want anyone to stir up trouble, not even your own people. Hinkston's dreams of empire would have been bad enough, what with him burning other operators and making himself noticeable, but then Dwight started killing people. Even so, I figure the capper was Monday night, when Mancuso got shot."

"That prostitute, Becky, got shot, too."

"Yes, but you have to look at it from the mob's point of view. A wounded cop sends every other cop into a rage. The heat comes down on everyone; it costs money. And Manny

Hinkston was a nut case. There's no telling what he might have done under pressure.''

Hilda said, "So they simply killed him? A band of killers came all the way from Kansas City and *shot* him, just like that?''

"Yeah, although I'm only guessing about the Kansas City connection, because of what Mancuso said. They were out-of-towners, though. I think.''

"Why did they kill both of them? Wouldn't they have either blamed the boss—Hinkston—for everything or blamed the other man, Stapner, for stealing and causing the trouble?''

I said, "Up in Canada if a bear gets too aggressive and starts tearing up campsites and chasing people, the rangers shoot them. If it's a mother bear with cubs, they shoot the cubs, too. The cubs have been trained the wrong way, and there's no going back. Maybe that's why the mob whacked Hinkston *and* Dwight. And Burridge, too, for that matter.''

"What do you know about bears in Canada?''

"Couple of guys and I went camping up there years ago. We paddled canoes clear to hell and gone up a chain of lakes into a national forest. One morning mama bear chased us out of our own camp. So we spent the next night on an island with a bunch of nurses from Toronto.''

Hilda sighed. "I almost believed that until you got to the part about nurses.''

"Remind me to tell you that story sometime.''

Hilda sat quietly for a few moments, then she said, "How do your police friends feel about all this?''

"Beats me. I haven't talked to them.''

"But . . .''

"Ducello and I made a deal. The problem's solved now. Ed Durkee can live without knowing all the details. Besides, when Cowboy and I went over there, we were going after Hinkston and Dwight. I didn't intend to phone Ed this morning and say, 'Guess who I shot last night.' ''

"You didn't say anything about a deal with, uh, Ducello. You said you were pointing guns at each other.''

"We didn't spell it out, but there was an understanding.''

Hilda said softly, "Is that why they didn't kill you and Cowboy? Because of your understanding?"

"Partly. And partly because Cowboy and I take a lot of killing. They'd have taken heavy losses in the process. And then, too, Ducello wanted to show the other one, Paolo somebody, how people should act. With honor, he said. Ducello and I had a little something going there. Paolo was an outsider."

"Oh, God, not another macho male honor code."

I shrugged. "It worked. Gotta say that for it."

Hilda frowned for several blocks after that. Eventually she said, "Why is it so important we see Patty this afternoon?"

"It's a surprise. You'll see."

Two blocks from Patty's house, Hilda shifted in her seat to face me. "I'm glad you didn't kill those men. I don't like to think of you doing that."

"Yeah, I'm glad, too."

When I turned the corner onto the block where Patty lived, Hilda said, "What is that?"

"Not bad, eh?"

A black limousine was parked at the curb in front of Patty's house. I stopped behind it. The gray-jacketed chauffeur watched in his rearview mirror as Hilda and I got out of the Mustang.

As we went up the walk Patty and Fall-down Forester came out of her front door. Fall-down looked great; dynamite suit, subdued tie, slim black document case. Very classy.

Patty looked great, too. She was dressed up, but better yet, she had a wide proud smile, and she held her chin higher that I'd ever seen. "Oh, good," she said when she saw us. "Let me introduce Deputy Director Galsworthy."

Fall-down shook Hilda's hand with a patrician nod, then looked at me as if we'd never seen each other. "Oh, yes," he said, "Rafferty. We spoke on the telephone."

"Yes," I said. "Here's my full report." I handed him an envelope; he tucked it into his suit-coat breast pocket.

"Mr. Galsworthy told me all about Sherm's work," Patty bubbled. "He said the nicest things." She stepped closer to Hilda and me. "And they've awarded Sherm the most wonderful certificate. I'll show you later, inside."

Fall-down harrumphed. "But no one else, please, my dear. And then straight into the safety deposit box. There are security considerations."

"Oh, of course," Patty said. "I understand completely." She blinked her blue eyes and smiled at everything in sight.

Fall-down shifted his document case into his left hand and made a show of checking his watch. A Rolex. A fifty-dollar Hong Kong Rolex, no doubt, but it was a nice touch for a guy who usually works fake back-injury scams. "Hmm," he said, "I must get back to Washington."

We all walked Fall-down to the limo and watched the chauffeur settle him into the wide rear seat. "Thank you, Mr. Galsworthy," Patty said. "Thank you very much."

Fall-down nodded regally and motioned to the chauffeur to close the door.

After the limo had purred away, Patty turned to me. "And thank you, Mr. Rafferty. Until you phoned this morning, I had no idea what an exciting—Oh, Wilma! Excuse me!" She galloped next door to Mrs Holmiston's house and pushed the doorbell.

Hilda looked up at me, squinting into the sun. "Was that money in the envelope you gave him?"

"Three hundred bucks," I said. "I put the limo on MasterCard."

"You fool," she said, grinning.

"What the hell. The Mustang doesn't really need new rings yet."

"I love you," she said.

"Shows you got great taste, cookie."

Then Patty and Mrs. Holmiston came back, heads together, walking and talking rapidly. "Come in," Patty said to us. "You have to see Sherm's certificate. Oh, and I baked this morning, Mr. Rafferty. The apple pie you like."

Hilda put her arm around my waist as we followed the chatting women. "How about I sit next to you, big fella?" she said. "You look like my kind of guy."

So we went inside, ate apple pie, and talked about what a wonderful fellow Sherm Akister had been.

ABOUT THE AUTHOR

W. GLENN DUNCAN, a former newsman and professional pilot, has lived in Iowa, Ohio, Oregon, Florida, Texas, and California. He now lives with his wife and three children in Australia. His previous novels are RAFFERTY'S RULES, RAFFERTY: LAST SEEN ALIVE, RAFFERTY: POOR DEAD CRICKET, and RAFFERTY: WRONG PLACE, WRONG TIME.